Girl Writer

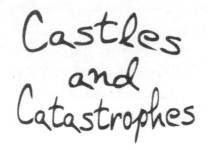

Castles
and
Catastrophes

Girl Writer

Castles
and
Catastrophes

Ros Asquith

PICCADILLY PRESS • LONDON

For day dreamers everywhere, with love

First published in Great Britain in 2006
by Piccadilly Press Ltd.,
5 Castle Road, London NW1 8PR
www.piccadillypress.co.uk

A catalogue record for this book is available
from the British Library

ISBN-10: 1 85340 823 9 (trade paperback)
ISBN-13: 978 1 85340 823 6

3 5 7 9 10 8 6 4 2

Printed and bound in Great Britain by Bookmarque Ltd
Cover illustration by Bernice Lum
Cover design by Simon Davis

Set in 11.25 point Novarese Book and 11.5 point TylersHand

Prologues, Palindromes and Pangrams

Dear Readers and Writers,

A prologue, as everybody knows, is the bit of the book at the front that introduces it. Prologues can be dull, but this one is very IMPORTANT, because if you do read it you could win a PRIZE!

I'll let you into a secret: I want to be an author. I want to tell stories for as long as I live. The greatest moment for every famous author is their first literary success, when they realise that, yes, they will make it as a writer. That moment came for me last year, when I was eleven years old, with my story, *The Lady of the Rings*. At the time I was also writing a diary which I called *The Story of My Life*. I have put highlights from them both together for you here so you can see how my greatest moment came about.

Hopefully one day my writing will make me very rich and famous, and if you'd also like to be an author, you'll find lots of tips for how to do it that might make you rich and famous too – though of course not as r and f as me, do you take me for a fuel? Some tips I've learned from my aunt, Laura Hunt. She's a famous writer of books for young people, though personally I think one or two of them could do with a bit of improvement (the books, not the young people).

All writers use words – just like painters use paint. And all of these words are made up (in English anyway) of just twenty-six letters! Imagine that. Shakespeare used the same twenty-six letters that you and I can use.

I love playing with words, and before you read on I'm going to tell you about some interesting kinds of words. Not only can you look out for them in my writing, but they'll also make you sound a real brainiac if you drop them into the conversation.

A palindrome, for instance, is a word or sentence that is the same spelled forward or backward. If your name is Anna, or Bob, or Niffin, or Vumxglylgxmuv, then you are lucky to have a name that is a palindrome. 'Mum' and 'Dad' are palindromes too, which may mean that babies are more clever than we think because those are the first words they say. My favourite palindrome is the one for waiters and wait-resses: *Stressed? No tips? Spit on desserts.* (Read it again and you'll see it works.)

I should also tell you about spoonerisms. This is when the first letters of words get mixed up; for instance, a 'half-formed wish' becomes a 'half-warmed fish'. You'll see that one of my teachers makes these amusing bungles sometimes . . . but I think she does it on purpose, to keep us on our toes.

A pangram is a sentence that contains all the letters of the alphabet. Here are two examples: *The quick brown fox jumps over the lazy dog.* (I bet some of you knew that one.) *Pack my box with five dozen liquor jugs.* (Bet you didn't know that one.)

Now you know what a pangram is, keep an eye out for one hidden within my wonderful story, *The Lady of the Rings.* Remember, it has to be a SINGLE SENTENCE. You will also find a palindrome too. You will have to read it all to find them. Heh! Heh! (That's the sound of insane laughter coming from my bedroom garret, where I write of love, art, hoodies and banshees.)

The first five readers to spot the pangram AND the palindrome correctly will win twenty pounds worth of books from ye fab Piccadilly Press. Write to me, Cordelia Arbuthnott (or e-mail books@piccadillypress.co.uk) at Piccadilly Press, 5 Castle Road, London, NW1 8PR.

Good luck!

Love,

Cordelia Lucinda Arbuthnott, or perhaps

C.L. Arbuthnott, or

Cordy Arb, or

CLA

(Must decide which one looks best on my book jacket.)

P.S. You can read highlights from *The Lady of the Rings*, the book I was writing last year, at the end of each chapter. It is all about this Romantic, Fevered, Tragic Heroine stuff. Or you can skip it, and just read *The Story of My Life*. If you read them both, you can ask yourself the question I keep asking myself, and haven't found the answer to yet. Which is better? Fact or fiction?

You are also getting TWO BOOKS FOR THE PRICE OF ONE.

Chapter One

Author or Bust

I have just found an old letter I wrote to Father Christmas in Candice's 'special things' drawer. I can't imagine how it got there because I swear I saw it go up the chimney all those years ago when I was six. But it proves one thing to me for certain: I was born to write.

Deer Santer,
I wood lik Fury Barbie horse wiv wings.
A bisicle.
A leaf.

A lion.
Pink ink and proper quill pens.
Parchment.
Trayners wiv lites on.
A book wiv lessens on how to be a famus riter lik mi aunt,
Laura Hunt.
Luv to Rudelf.
From yor fan, Cordelia.

See? I couldn't spell well, but I could spell *parchment* and *quill*. I've always liked old stuff, even back then. I wonder if Rudolph minded about me spelling his name wrong? Or maybe there was a rude elf in Santa's band of little helpers who got really cheered up by my message because I was the only person who was ever nice to him?

I'm still trying to be a writer nearly six whole years later. So far I've written:

Lots of beginnings and lots of endings,

Twelve poems,

Woof – a short book about dogs,

Ant Girl – a long book about a girl who has been shrunk and is trying to find the cure,

Three Bees Go Boating – for the Three Bees (that's Aunt Laura's grandchildren: Bessie, Bertie and Bobby). They are only three so they haven't read my story yet but Aunt Laura says she has read it to them six times.

Aunt Laura is my dad's big sister. She is twelve years older than my dad and had her own children ridiculously young, which is how she got to be a granny already. She is also the bestselling children's author Laura Hunt, whose website has fantastic 'tips for budding authors' which are going to make me a megastar too.

My dream is to become a bestselling author between now and next Monday. That's when I start my repulsive new school, Falmer North. So only the lottery, suicide, a fatal accident, kidnap, spontaneous combustion – that's quite a lot of things already – but, most likely, bestselling authoring can save me now.

Can you be rocketed to fame and fortune that quickly? I don't see why not – look at *Big Brother*.

My major trouble is that, until this summer, I had three good friends and not ONE of them is going to Falmer North. Meg has gone home to Ireland. Emily is going to St Hilda's and Callum, my best friend in all the world, is going to Arlington Oratory, the boys' school. I begged and begged my parents to send me to St Hilda's, but they just said they weren't made of money. I can see they're not made of money, obviously – they are made of bones and bits of skin, like everyone else. But I got the point and felt spoiled for asking. You may find this odd, if you have thought about these things, but I was really shocked. I never knew you had actually to pay money for some schools. I did know Candice (that's my mum) wanted me to go to a 'good' school and I did the exam for Barnaby High and I FAILED. All the clever kids from my old primary school got in there. But then they all had tutors and I didn't.

Candice used to go on and on about how she couldn't possibly send me to Falmer North because it was full of 'hoodies and banshees'. She meant scary boys in hoodies and scary girls who scream with laughter, shout rude words and drop litter all up the road. She said nobody wants to send their kids to Falmer North because it has a 'reputation'. But now, because there is No Alternative, she is trying to be falsely bright and make out like it will be OK. The result of all this parental worrying about 'standards' and 'drugs' and 'hoodies and banshees' is that I am honestly scared stiff, like a stiff, scared thing. I used my fabled imagination and came up with the brilliant idea of dressing up as a boy and going to Arlington Oratory with Callum, but it turns out you have to pay for THAT school too, so all my hopes and dreams have come to naught . . . I would make a good boy though – I'm short and scrawny and could get a short scrawny wig to match.

I am dreading, dreading, dreading Falmer North. But if I can make stacks of money like my Aunt Laura does, just from writing a few old books and putting them in pink sparkly covers, then I could afford to go to St Hilda's with Emily. YES! Or at least afford a tutor to get me in somewhere nice. I am really one of those kids who would like to be home educated, allowing me plenty of time to run free, climb trees, write poetry and gaze dreamily at the sky. I did suggest this.

'How on earth could I possibly find time to home educate

you?' asked Candice, looking anxious and guilty. 'You know I'd love to, darling, but the gallery takes every available moment . . .'

'I could do it myself. At the library,' I said.

Candice sighed tragically in reply.

So it's Falmer North for me, and it IS scary. But there is one ray of hope: Candice told me she heard some kind parent has given the school money for a writing competition 'to encourage the Year Sevens in a love of literature'.

So now I am determined to win. I have been plotting an olde-fashioned romance with knights and ladies and castles and dragons and horses and murder and adventure. I don't want to read any more books about problems with school, or friends, or miserable families. I get enough of all that in real life.

I want to ESCAPE, reach for the stars and all that. So here goes. Before I write, I often check out my dear old Aunt Laura's writer's tips.

Laura Hunt's Top Tips for Budding Writers:
If you're not sure how to start, try looking at the opening lines of some of your favourite books.

Not helpful. Oliver Twist starts with 'Among other public buildings in a certain town'. The first Harry Potter book begins with stuff about Privet Drive.

I start a lovely clean page. I dip my pen in my purple ink . . .
The Lady of the Rings: Volume One.

Phew. Have written out the whole title. Knackered
already.

I must break off from my exhausting task of writing for a
quick MIRROR CHECK, just so you can get to know me
better.

I don't know why I do this. It's always the same. I've never
looked in the mirror and seen the Goddess of My Dreams
smiling back at me, but I live in hope she'll turn up one day
and take me away from all this, i.e. Me.

Resemblance to Lady Cordelia (the heroine of The
Greatest Novel Ever Written): nil.

Hair: lank and beige. Beige like a mushroom, and also
mushroom-like in being flat, boring, clammy, dome-shaped

thing drooping around a straight-up-and-down stem, which is more or less the shape of my body. No hot, fevered, heaving bosoms or anything along those lines. And I don't want any either, you can bet on that.

Neck: Unswan-like. Trussed chicken, maybe?

Come to think of it, how did I get ink on my neck? What a ridiculous person I am. Maybe I should start writing my novel on the computer instead of with the fabled fountain pen given to me by Candice in hopes of fulfilling my natural genius.

Why don't I just call Candice 'Mum', like any normal person, I hear you ask? Because she doesn't want me to. She says, when you go to the supermarket and someone shouts 'Mum' at least half the women turn their heads. She says she ought to be addressed as an individual, not a category. That's all very well, though I'm worried it might lead to people at Falmer North putting me into a category for calling my mum Candice, and that category is Weird, which nobody nearly twelve years old wants to be in. Candice says it's OK to be different and that all the best people are different. But I think maybe I'm a bit *too* different, what with being called Cordelia, looking like a boy and wanting to write books about faire ladies and gentil knights rather than hang out with all those scary boys in hoodies at Falmer North. Anyway, got distracted, as usual. Back to Mirror Check.

Dress? Excellent. Green velvet. Colour of emeralds? No, tinned peas. Amazing amount of ink stains too.

Knees: horrible. Scabs all over, like boys' knees. Should I stop tree-climbing with Callum now I am starting at vile Falmer North?

Callum is the lifelong best friend in all the world that I mentioned earlier. If I was born to write, then he was born to draw. You should see his pictures. He is going to be the illustrator of my book, if only I can get him to draw faire ladies instead of superheroes. I don't want The Lady Cordelia Arbuthnott looking like the Incredible Hulk. Callum's parents are my parents' best friends, so Callum and I have been hanging out together since before we could walk. We went to playgroup together, then primary school. Callum can wiggle his ears. I used to nod, knowingly, as if he was sending me secret messages in code; everyone used to crowd round and ask what he was saying. We made it all up, of course. Callum turned out to be dyslexic later, so people still have trouble understanding him, only now it's when he's writing stuff. Poor Callum.

However, not Poor Callum today. Our Lifelong Friendship is under threat. He said he'd be here at nine-thirty to go swimming if it was warm enough – and it's actually quite hot today. It's our last few days of freedom, before I start foul Falmer North and he goes swanning off to snotty Arlington Oratory, so how can he be late? (Apart from the fact that he's always late, of course.)

I've just noticed that I've written Falmer North about a million times. Am I obsessed? Perhaps I am getting school phobia and can get a sick note about not going. If my book doesn't work out, that could be the best option. Nothing for it but to return to The Greatest Novel Ever Written.

I was honestly about to put pen to paper when I heard the familiar BRING, BRING, BRING of our own dear old telephone.

'CORDELIA!!!'

'WHAT??' quoth I, rather crossly.

'Callum ON THE PHONE!'

Reluctantly leaving The Greatest Novel Ever Written, I went downstairs to the phone.

'I don't know why he doesn't call your mobile,' Candice said.

'Yes, you do,' I replied. 'It's because you encouraged me to be a dreamy, impractical person who can't remember to ever charge her battery.'

'Anyone would think you didn't want to talk to people,' Candice said, shrugging. She went back to helping Howard (that's my dad) find his glasses before going out to work. This is a challenge in our house. Firstly, none of us knows how to tidy up. Secondly, every surface is covered with pots and bowls and jugs from Candice's ceramics gallery and all these pots and bowls and jugs like to eat missing wallets, homework and glasses. I don't know why she doesn't say to Howard, 'Anyone would think you didn't want to see people.' He's a college lecturer in medieval English, so if he doesn't have his glasses he can't see the notes of the lecture he's giving (and probably has given ever since it really was medieval times), Alas Alack and Woe Is Him. But then hopefully he also can't see all the students that will probably be texting each other or falling asleep.

My folks are, honestly, a bit eccentric. I suppose they are 'arty'. Howard is round and balding and cuddly and wears moth-eaten pullovers and tweedy jackets like fathers in olde books. He is dreamy and constantly looks mildly surprised, like a teddy bear who has just found out he has to give lectures and talk to students when all he really wants is to gaze into space or hang out with other teddies at the odd picnic. Candice is always trying to tidy him up, though she can't tidy herself up and dashes out of the house with her arms full of pottery, her scarf trailing behind her and her bag undone. She is tall and thin and anxious and always in a hurry. On this occasion she was so busy looking for Howard's glasses that she'd neglected to notice that she'd dropped the receiver in Xerxes's bowl. I fished it out.

'Hello, Clammy, where are you?' I said to the silence I assume is full of Callum at the other end.

'Prithee, standing opposite thy noble doss-house,' Callum's voice replied. It is really sweet how he has started talking like my book. For weeks now, ever since I got that faint ray of hope about the writing competition, he's been trying to encourage me to get on with my Medieval Romance by doing this daft medieval-speak to get me in the mood. Or ye moode.

'Thou buffoon,' I said, peering into the street from the hall, and there Callum certainly was, skulking behind a tree with his mobile to his ear.

'Thou mewling pox-marked vassal,' he replied.

'I thought we were going swimming, thou paunchy milk-livered lout,' I said, sticking one thumb in my ear and my tongue out at Callum, but he couldn't see me. Xerxes, our lazy old cat could though, and hissed in retaliation before wandering off grumpily into the kitchen. 'It's our last days of freedom.' (The cat didn't say that, I did.)

'Come outside, I've got to talk to you,' Callum said. He sounded different to usual, so I said yes at once.

'Candice, I'm going swimming with Callum!'

'That's right, abandon us when Howard's having the worst glasses crisis ever,' came a distant, distracted voice. As I ran upstairs to collect my swimming things, something glinting caught my eye on the telephone table in the hall.

'They're in the fish tank. Byeee,' I called, running downstairs again. Glasses in fishtanks. Phones in cat bowls. My parents are really very strange, I thought to myself as I went out the front door. I made a mental note to buy a friend for Blue, the goldfish. He gets so excited when things happen, like glasses falling into his tank, and of course he doesn't get out and about much. He must be lonely.

Callum was pacing up and down by a tree.

'The worst thing in the world is happening,' Callum said, almost before I got within earshot.

'You're dying of the dreaded flowering-willy syndrome, one of nature's cruellest jokes,' I suggested. 'Or your dyslexia's spread to your feet so you don't know what direction you're going in. Your mum's cut her head off with a designer kitchen appliance. Your dad woke up to find he was a giant herbivore.'

'Worse than all that. He's got a secret girlfriend.'

That shut me up.

'Are you sure?' I said eventually.

'Well, I'm hoping I'm wrong,' replied Callum.

'But your dad's old and fat,' I said, without thinking. I didn't understand for a moment why Callum looked so hurt. 'That's good, isn't it?' I continued quickly. 'It makes it less likely that he has a girlfriend.'

'I thought you LIKED my dad,' Callum said quietly.

'I LOVE your dad,' I protested. 'I've known him since before I was born. Well, you know what I mean. My dad and yours went to school together, got married in the same week – not to each other, of course. Your dad's, like, my dad's oldest friend. And my mum and your mum too.'

It's true. Callum's folks, Peter and Andrea, have been best pals with my folks forever. We're almost like the same family, except they've got about five times the amount of money we've got.

'Anyway, I'm sure he does have a girlfriend,' Callum groaned.

'He can't have. Therapists don't DO things like that. They know what damage it causes families,' I told him brightly, not feeling very convinced. Callum's dad may spend his time trying to help people, but he earns a fortune and when I thought about it, Howard always says men with money can afford girlfriends, unlike poor university lecturers like him.

Callum kicked the tree. 'He has. I know he has.'

'How do you know?'

'He's got a funny look in his eye.'

'He always had. He squints.' I could feel myself digging a deep hole. I tried to make it better. 'At least your dad can see with his own two eyes though, even if they are looking in different directions – Howard's always running around moaning he can't find his glasses.'

I became aware of Callum looking as if he was about to attack me.

'Sorry,' I said, meekly. 'Honest, I love Peter. And your mum. Andrea and Peter get on really well. He wouldn't do anything to hurt her, surely?'

'He's always on the phone when Mum's out these days,' Callum went on. 'Then he starts whispering or hangs up if I come in the room. He's been writing a lot of e-mails too, but I can't read them without knowing his password. And he's been sending off letters in fancy coloured envelopes. I offered to post one when I was going out yesterday, and he got all shifty and said he'd do it. What does all that mean if it isn't a girlfriend? It's just like how people go behind each other's backs on TV.'

I pondered on this for a bit as we set off to the beach. Callum is certainly very oversensitive just now. Maybe he is falling in love with me. I expect that's it. It often happens with really close friends at about this age. Maybe it is not quite right to have a boy as a best friend now I am becoming mature. Maybe I should try to get to know some girls at my new school. Maybe there will be another budding writer, like me, who will understand my true inner depth.

Callum interrupted my thoughts.'You wouldn't like it if your mum or dad was seeing someone else.'

My mum or dad? Don't make me laugh.

Despite Callum's worries, we still had an excellent morning on the beach – just like the old days.

After our swim we dug a hole in the pebbly bit of the beach and covered it with a plank that had washed up. Then we found some tough washing line that we attached to the plank, smothered the lot with pebbles and seaweed and just lay back to watch.

'Where have you got to in your book?" Callum asked.

I quoted a few lines and Callum looked at me with awe.

'Thou rapturous elfin-fingered artiste,' he murmured.

'Odds bodkins, Old Lady Alert!' I responded, seeing a couple of anciente crones tottering dangerously towards our booby trap.

Old Lady Alert means one of us has to stand by the trap looking at the sky, as if it was painted by Picasso or something, so the old lady has to step round us, clucking crossly (could evolution have it wrong, and actually we're all descended from chickens, not apes?) and not fall in, so avoiding breaking every bone in her body and getting us hung, drawn and quartered for senior citizen abuse. Kids never fall in of course – they jump right over it; they can smell a booby trap like dogs smell bones.

'You're going to be a great writer, you know,' Callum

whispered after I came back and we were lying very still (except Callum's ears, which twitched gently – I wonder if he knows they do that? I'm afraid all that practice at primary school might have damaged his nervous system) and we concentrated all our psychic powers on the seaweed, and making it an irresistible lure for the next passerby.

Some poser in lime-green swim shorts and mirror shades turned up, trying to chat up three girls who were shrieking with laughter at his jokes, but not meaning it. Callum fingered the rope.

'I envy you being able to do that,' he said to me. 'Whatever your worries are, you can always put it right in a story.'

'But it's not real life,' I said. 'I spend more time thinking up stories than anyone I know, but even I know it isn't the same as real life.'

'It's true,' said Callum, looking up now as Lime-green Shorts approached the point of no return. 'Wrong stuff in life can be hard to fix.'

Lime-green Shorts paused to flex his sinews and flick his hair at the trio of girlies.

'Now!' said Callum, pulling the rope. The plank skidded away from under the seaweed and Lime-green Shorts dropped neatly into the hole. He began squeaking and hopping up and down, to the hysterical giggles of the girlies.

'Hope that jellyfish wasn't still alive,' said Callum, as we ran for it, giggling hysterically ourselves.

'Callum! You didn't put a jellyfish in that hole did you?'

When we'd put some distance between us and the scene of the crime, we looked back. Then Callum looked at me.

'Do you think we're getting too old for this kind of thing?' he asked.

'Nah,' we both said at the same time, and doubled up laughing.

'Your hovel or mine?' I said, when I'd recovered.

We went back to my place as Callum wanted to hear the beginning of The Greatest Novel Ever Written. Candice met us in the hall.

'Look at the state of you two,' she said. 'Aren't you getting a bit old for this kind of thing?'

But I want to stay eleven forever. I want to climb trees and dream and have adventures. I don't want to be forced to wear high heels and nose studs and be a ladette before my time.

I spotted Candice smiling a rueful smile. I think she wants me to stay a little girl too, sometimes. She proved it by bringing us banana milkshakes and a plate of biscuits up into my room, where Callum had snuggled under my duvet to read my book. He looked about six and I made a mental note that if, unlikely as it is, I make any friends at Falmer North, I had better change my Postman Pat duvet before I ask them home. And how many kids my age still fit into their Angelina Ballerina pyjamas?

'It's good stuff this,' Callum said, deep in *The Lady of the Rings*. Lucky he is a slow reader, as it is exactly a page long so far. He seemed to have forgotten his worries for a while. Books can do that to you, maybe even my book can.

'I wish you could tell me how to start,' he said. 'I'd like to write one too.'

'Ah,' said I. 'Forsooth. That's another story.'

Callum seemed a bit cheerier when he went home, but I found myself getting all hot and bothered at the thought of his folks splitting up. What would we do at Christmas? And in the summer? Our two families always do holidays together . . . I can't afford to lose Callum, especially now I am plunging into the dreade new cesspit of Falmer North.

I will lose myself in my art yette againe. Soone I will be so loste that no one will find me and then I will not have to go to ye sinke school of ye centurye, while Callum swans off to wear blazers and play cricket with MPs' sons at Arlington Oratory.

Quick writer's tip check to get me in ye moode againe.

Laura Hunt's Top Tips for Budding Writers:
Don't go into too much character detail
at first.

Erm, so mustn't put, 'Emma Woodhouse, handsome, clever, and rich, with a comfortable home and happy disposition,' like Jane Austen did.

Well, I've written loads tonight and I've talked enough about it, so I'm sure you can't wait to get a taste of The Greatest Novel Ever Written, begun that very week and written just as I originally wrote it, with all my deep writerly thoughts included.

The Lady of the Rings

'Alas, alack and woe is me! The end is nigh, unless I flee!'

Princess Duchess Madam The Lady Cordelia Arbuthnott threw back her swan-like, ivory-white neck and threw her shining, luminous, lustrous eyes to the heavens. (They made a loud boing sound as they hit the bejewelled ceiling of her boudoir, bounced off the head of the stuffed aardvark on the wall and fell into the fish tank, disturbing the two piranhas, Eric and Ernie, who swallowed them in a flash, briefly turning the water into a tumult of boiling red, and knocking over the plastic lighthouse on the bottom.)

'Woe is me a thousand times more!' quoth The Lady Cordelia. 'How will I see my way to flee now?' (I must take my story seriously, or no one else will. But it's so easy to get distracted when you're an author, and there's no teacher glaring at you telling you to sit up and concentrate ... Phew, this is hard work already. Where was I? Ah yes, 'throwing her lustrous eyes to the heavens'.)

'Alas, alack and woe is me,' cried The Lady Cordelia Arbuthnott, again and again, hoping that the youthful and finely-chiselled form of Lothario, her devoted Italian stallion of a manservant, would come to her aid. 'Gadzooks! Is he deaf?' (Did anyone ever understand what this poomplex language meant? Note to self: must remember to check if ever used in olde books. Or is it just gibberish to convey ancientness? In period novels it's very important to get the language right. Maybe thirtieth-century authors will be throwing in 'wicked' and 'awesome' all over the place to convey the long-lost era of the twenty-first century, if the planet hasn't been flooded by global warming or hit by an asteroid by then. Meanwhile, back in the twelfth century ...)

She tossed her tumultuous mane of golden curls, which normally grew all down her back, but today stood out in a frenzy of alarm, as it always did when The Lady Cordelia's seventh sense, famed throughout the kingdom for its magical, mysteriouse, mystic powers, sensed PERIL.

Ever since cock-crow, the toads had been croaking ominously in the moat. The Black Swan of Deth had been circling the castle, making whatever noise it is swans make. (I wish I knew more about stuff like that, I should pay more attention in science lessons.) The seagulls had been flying, whirring amid the throng of twisted, gnarled, scabrous trees in the Enchanted Forest and even in the very heavens, hanging ominously low and threatening over the jagged, melancholy, misty mountains, the dark clouds almost scraped themselves against the narrow stained glass window through which The Lady Cordelia peered in deep dismay, aghast. Dimly, through the gathering fog, she perceived, as if in a darkening nightmare, a knight-mare indeed. (Hah! Excellent word play, forsooth ...)

'Twas the faint figure of a young man bedecked in glittering armour astride an exquisitely dappled palomino steed, galloping, galloping, galloping, ever closer. She could discern, encircling his noble brow, brighter than his shimmering golden curls, a shimmering golden crown, like as those worn by Zeus and Kubla Khan from Xanadu and other olde fogies embedded with precious shimmering gems. (Erm, maybe it would be too hard to see this much detail through mist, fogge and portents ... maybe re-write to make it a sunny day?)

'Alas, it is true. A prince comes. I am undone!' she cried, fiddling frantically with her hundreds of pearl buttons while tearing at the bejewelled pendulum that encircled her noble swan-like neck and beating her strong, womanly, richly-bejewelled fists against her angry, hot, scalding, fevered breasts. She drew her precious amulet to her snowy breast and scooped up her paintbrush with the other.

'I WILL NOT marry a prince. Not this one, not that one, not another one, nor anyone! They are all of them, dissembling, clay-brained codpieces!' she announced to her faithful, though youthful, Italian manservant who did her every bidding and was just now attending to her duvet. 'I was born for better things,' bellowed The Lady Cordelia. 'I was born to be an artist! I LIVE for my art. I will DIE for my art.'

(That's more like it. Not sure about dying for art, but people carried on like this a lot more Back In The Day, and they probably didn't mean it. Anyway, they died so fast of plagues, invading hordes, ravening wolves, witchcraft and such things, that it probably wasn't such a big deal to bang on about it.)

Laura Hunt's Top Tips for Budding Writers:

End each chapter on a cliffhanger.

Must bring a cliff into next bit.

But ye prince on ye horizon – I think I'll call him Prince Kevin – was The Lady Cordelia's very own Falmer North. I should maybe have just packed my bags and fled, or fainted into a frenzy on my Postman Pat duvet. In my Angelina Ballerina pyjamas. But considering it was the dreade starte of school the next day, and with all the interruptions I'd had, it wasn't bad for a first bash.

Chapter Two

Ye Dreaded New Schoole

Laura Hunt's Top Tips for Budding Writers:
Try to make your images original, rather than using tired phrases such as 'white as snow' or 'as cold as ice'. (These are called clichés.)

This makes me mad as a hatter. Or maybe daft as a brush. What do I say instead? Her cheeks were as white as snowballs? A bride's dress? (But not those creamy ones.) Bird droppings? Anyway, am determined to avoid clichés like the plague.

So. How would I describe Falmer North? Did it make me miserable as sin? Fill me with fear and loathing? Grip me with an icy fear? No. I was beyond all that. It was my first day. The dread day that seemed so far away at the beginning of the summer has now ended. I was early. Goodness knows why. Why would anyone want to get to horrible Falmer North early? It's the writer in me. I must have subconsciously wanted to take in The Scene. Absorb the atmosphere. Feel the pain . . . I wanted to run like the wind in the other direction, but I knew I had to go through with it.

Disgusting Falmer North. Not only are there no moats, spires, turrets, drawbridges, talking portraits, crazed, limping janitors with hunched backs, beards and leers, there aren't even any playing fields and not even a proper uniform.

And I didn't know anyone except Zandra and Jolene, who I've known, in a don't-want-to-know sort of way, almost as long as Callum. For some reason known only to the people who design these great big child-chewing schools, Zandra and Jolene are the only girls from my old school who are in my new class.

Zandra and Jolene! The very words strike terror deep within the soul. Callum says he still wakes up screaming when he dreams about them playing spin the bottle at their seventh birthday party and swarming all over him with wet, sloppy kisses. He said he'd never realised until then that falling into a tankful of giant squid might be better than being kissed. I think it may have damaged him permanently – he's sworn never to let himself be kissed again, ever. I hope he doesn't have to spend a lot of money on a psychiatrist in later life, what with that and the ear-wiggling thing – and now everything else.

Candice told me not to worry about Zandra and Jolene. She said they have probably never read a book, not even one of Aunt Laura's. I am beginning to wonder if Candice is a bit of a snob, but she is the only mum I have got, so I don't want to think about it too much. Anyway, it's good if Z and J haven't read a book. It means they won't read mine, which also means it'll be all right using them for inspiration when it comes to the Evil Sisters I intend to introduce in the sequel. They suffocate unsuspecting princes in surprise kissing attacks, but end up being turned into stone by a witch. No, hang on, I've read that somewhere else – *Narnia*. The being turned to stone, I mean, not the kiss attacks. Drat! Every good idea I have seems to be someone else's. On the other hand, that turning to stone thing is done by gorgons in Greek myths too, so I guess nothing is exactly original. Maybe they could be turned into octopuses. Or eaten by octopuses in an underwater café where Zandra soufflé and jellied Jolene are all the rage.

Anyway, it wasn't too long before other people started to arrive. I didn't recognise anyone. They looked at me a bit strangely, I think. As I feared, the boys were all in hoodies and a lot of the girls were swanning about with crop-tops and lots of belly piercings. I had hoped there would be at least some parents from nice, decent, poor homes who would send their kids off like Candice suggested, in 'proper school clothes' and that I might just blend in with the school outfit she bought me at M&S.

I did not blend. And this was not just because nobody else was wearing a white shirt, grey jacket, grey skirt and socks . . .

After a special Year Seven assembly – all about being

welcome at our new school, respect, not wearing baseball caps in class, using mobile phones in lessons, chewing gum, putting gum under desks, carving names on pupils, desks (sorry, used comma instead of apostrophe) and so on – we had our first science lesson with our nice new form tutor, Mrs Warren.

At least she is old-fashioned and cosy-looking and looks like one of the flopsy bunnies from Beatrix Potter, with her large front teeth, long ears, wrinkly nose and, yes, I'm sorry to report, whiskery chin. I got all excited by seeing real test tubes and thought I could use the dangerous proximity of the bunsen burners to casually remove my grey jacket, which was making me feel like something out of *Just William*. I started subtly pulling my shirt out of my skirt in an effort to look more like the fashionistas when there was a roar of laughter so loud it almost broke the windows.

I looked round wildly. Had I missed the joke? Sadly, with everyone staring at me, it became clear it was me they were laughing at.Why? Why?

'Watch yer back', 'Hot shirt!', were just a couple of the remarks I could make out amid the caterwauling.

'Some of you have very mad banners, I hope you won't taste two worms fooling about, like my last Year Seven,' said Mrs Warren, winking at me.

The girl sitting next to me wasn't laughing though. She had long, fair hair and dreamy eyes, which were giving me a sweet, sympathetic look. She scribbled a note: *Big scorch mark on your back*. No wonder Candice helped me into my jacket so enthusiastically this morning. She'd obviously left the iron on my shirt, probably whilst sighing and pouring herself a reviving glass of something alcoholic.

I struggled back into my jacket while Mrs Warren shut everyone up with an exciting display of some gas or other which turned blue and fizzed, then exploded. Pretty cool move for Year Sevens on the first day. She may well get respect for this.

I tried to speak to the kind, fair-haired girl at the end of the lesson, but she had a strange keep-away kind of atmosphere around her that seemed to say, 'Don't come near me.' She shoved all her books in her bag, then skittered off like a frightened vole without meeting my eye. But I noticed that one of the books she shoved away was by Laura Hunt, and another was by Jane Austen.

I looked for the Mystery Girl at break but she had vanished, so, left alone, The Writer In Me took over. I imagined something else had happened entirely, that everyone had not been laughing at me, but had been speechless with amazement at my brilliant outfit. So I decided to play it like that.

Out of desperation I went to look for Zandra and Jolene, which normally wild horses wouldn't have dragged me to do.

'Hi,' I said. 'Wotcha think of the school?'

'Crap,' they both said at the same time, staring at their mobiles and texting away. 'But then they're all crap. Some of the boys are fit, though. The older ones.' They nudged each other, giggling.

'You still see Callum?' Zandra asked me.

'Yes. He's going to a private school now.'

'He was all right,' Jolene said. 'Bit of a nerd, but all right. Probably get more nerdy now, though. Dyspeptic, wasn't he?'

'Dyslexic,' I said.

'Shame, innit? Stead of being brilliant like us. What chance has he got?' They seemed to find this idea so funny I thought Zandra and Jolene were going to fall over laughing.

'I can see why you were laughing at me back in class,' I began.

'Oh yeah, that.' Jolene gave me a big push in the ribs, but it was meant to be quite a playful one. I think.

'How d'you get Cordelia's mum to burn her own ear?' Jolene asked Zandra, chortling.

'Ring her up while she's doing the ironing!' shouted Zandra, clearly on her wavelength and now in hysterics.

Oh. Ha ha.

'In actual fact,' I said, dramatically, 'my cousin, who is best friends with Kate Moss, modelled this exact same shirt in Berlin.'

There was a long silence, and Zandra and Jolene looked at me as if they weren't sure if I was mad.

'You serious?' asked Zandra.

'Sure. Like ripped jeans and headphones printed on T-shirts, this is where cutting edge design is currently at. I can get them at a quarter of the real price, too, but you're probably not interested, so who cares?' I said, and walked away.

At lunchtime Mrs Warren asked me if I was all right. 'The others weren't teasing you too much about your, er, shirt, dear, were they?' she said in that very kind voice that, unfortunately, makes you want to cry because it's so sympathetic. She offered me a tissue.

'In case you want to know your blows,' she said, winking again.

'It's all right. Candice just left the iron on it. My shirt, not my nose,' I told her. Mrs Warren looked a bit surprised. I realise now she probably thought Candice was our illegal immigrant servant. (Maybe I'll call Candice 'Mum' from now on in company.) 'But it's OK.' I was having trouble carrying on, because Mrs Warren looked so like a rabbit it was hard to concentrate. 'I told the others it was a designer thing hot off the London fashion shows.'

'Well done, Cordelia,' said Mrs Warren. 'You have turned a potential calamity into a success. You are proving that the glass is half full.'

'I'm sorry?'

'The optimist sees the bright side of everything, while the pessimist sees the worst,' Mrs Warren explained. 'To the optimist, a half glass of water is always half full. To the pessimist it is always half empty. Now run along or you'll hiss mystery.'

I'm sure this might have been wise, but just found myself thinking, Supposing the glass is completely full? And then you drink it all?

* * *

When the bell finally went at the end of school, it was like what happens when you open a cupboard that's crammed full of stuff and everything falls out at once. There are too many kids at Falmer North. Nearly all of them bigger than me. And no one else was wearing a shirt with an iron mark on the back.

I couldn't wait to get back to my room and The Greatest Novel Ever Written. Candice greeted me with a big, noisy hug and asked how it had gone. I told her it was all right.

'Are you sure, darling? You didn't get lost in all those horrid corridors? Or bullied? You weren't offered any drugs?' she said, her face crunched up with anxiety.

It is not easy to feel positive about my new school with a mum like mine. It was a relief to go up to my room, put on some music to get me in the mood and forget myself in my art.

At least, that was the plan. Two hours later and I had still not written a word. The story had come to a grinding halt and all my dreams of my name embossed on a book jacket (Silver on purple? Gold on crimson?) were as nothing. Images of Peter's dad snogging another woman and the banshees of Falmer North descending on me with steam irons were interrupting my creative flow.

It's at times like that I tend to ask Aunt Laura's advice about writing. Horrors! I wondered how long I could keep people at Falmer North from finding out Laura Hunt is my aunt? Or would it be worse if nobody knew or cared?

The thing that bothers me about Aunt Laura is that I'm not sure how good a writer she really is, despite all the books she sells. She always writes about 'issues', like she's trying to teach you a lesson. It's OK, but I know all that stuff – you get it on TV all the time – and great literature (of the kind I will write, of course) is about more than that, isn't it? What happened to hope, yearning, romance, tragedy, poetry, adventure and escape?

But there is something about Aunt Laura's writing that does occasionally get to me. Sometimes she seems to be talking straight to *me*, as I *really* am, and completely describes the way I feel inside.

I always print and keep all my e-mails from her. The last one went like this:

```
If you get stuck with a story, Cordy, try
writing in your diary. Sometimes what you
write in your diary can help you with a
```

story. But best of all, it is for you and
only you to read and you can pour out
your feelings and you don't have to worry
about how well you write it!

Do you know what Candice said when she read that? 'Typical of Laura to put an exclamation mark there. And wherever did she get the idea she could call you Cordy? So very mass market.'

'She's trying to be kind,' I said.

'Of course, she's lovely, dahling, we all love her distract-edly. But there's writing and writing. Anyone can write for the masses.'

Back in my room I wondered what she meant by that. Who are the masses? My new friends, not that I've made any yet, at Falmer North? And if it's so easy to sell books to them, why doesn't everybody do it? But my thoughts were shattered a few minutes later.

'CORDELIA!!' yelled Candice from downstairs. Maybe we need an intercom; she always sounds like she's telling people to get out of a burning building. 'CALLUM!!'

Callum was already opening my bedroom door by then.

'What the hell are you listening to?' he asked as he came in. 'Sounds like a funeral.' I'd forgotten I had my writing music on to drown out the dreary world.

'It's a funeral march,' I told him. 'A very fine piece of mood music for writing about the struggles and inner pain of The Lady Cordelia Arbuthnott.'

'It's a bit gloomy, just at the moment,' Callum said. I could see straightaway that his worries about his dad hadn't gone away.

He sat down on my bed and didn't say anything more. I was waiting for him to ask me about my first day at school.

'OK with your folks?' I asked in the end.

'All right.'

Another long silence.

'Girl Writer,' Callum eventually said to me, 'does writing help you . . . understand things?'

'A bit,' I told him. 'You sometimes have to think about why your characters act and feel the way they do. But at the moment I'm just concentrating on telling a good story.'

'Oh,' Callum said. He obviously wanted me to say something else.

'I think my Aunt Laura's the kind of writer you're thinking of,' I said. 'She writes a lot about feelings and . . . understanding things.'

Callum looked interested. He's known about Aunt Laura all our lives and even met her a few times, but this was the first time he'd ever shown any interest at all in what she actually does. It could be the sparkly pink book covers had put him off. Or the fact that in her books, no one ever gets eaten by sharks or disfigured by acid or rescued from towering infernos by young secret agents.

'What's her stuff like?' Callum asked.

I grabbed one of Laura's books at random off the shelf. It happened to be *Lost on the Way to Love*, which came out a couple of years ago. It's in Aunt Laura's older age range and has the words, Not *suitable for younger readers* on the back, which guarantees every ten-year-old will get their mitts on it if they can. But it's fairly tame compared to telly or girls' magazines.

I opened it at random and I read a bit out loud.

'"Oh my God," Freya said to Estelle. "I am just so stressed, it's unreal!"

'Estelle clicked off her walkman and gave her friend's arm a comforting squeeze.

'"Your dad again, huh?" she said. "You have to get things straight with him. Relationships change, you've just got to deal with it."

'"I handled him leaving us all," Freya said. "Those nights when he and Mum were screaming at each other were just so awful, and now at least that's over. But he hardly even calls me unless I call him first."

'"Maybe he feels guilty," Estelle suggested. "It's not that he doesn't love you."

'"He loves his new girlfriend, Anthea, more," said Freya in a very low voice. "And whenever I call, it's always her who answers the phone. 'Hi, sweetie,' she always says. 'What's happening?' I could kill her. She doesn't sound any older than me. Mum always asks if I've talked to her. Why does she want to torture herself?"'

'What do you think of it?' I asked Callum.

'It's OK,' he said slowly. He was very quiet, and I mentally cursed fate for picking a page about a dad leaving home for a girlfriend. I didn't realise until I had started reading, and then it would have been worse to draw attention to it and stop.

He suddenly perked up. 'It's not very exciting, but it'd be good if Freya and Estelle really did kill her dad's new girl-friend. But in those sort of books they just moan on about their feelings, instead of doing something about it.'

He stabbed my duvet with one of my many leaky blue biros as he said this. Right through Postman Pat's black and white cat. 'Black and Blue Cat now,' he added. 'Sorry.'

'Doesn't matter. I need a new cover anyway,' I said, relieved.

'Yeah. Wish I could write, though. I'd write about how Freya and Estelle realised, as one, what they had to do and murdered the girlfriend with a twelve-inch stainless steel kitchen knife or maybe shot her using a polished blue steel Ruger 77/50 Muzzleloader with a straight-gripped walnut stock, and rode off into the sunset with their long, bronzed legs astride an immaculately-restored 1968 Harley Electraglide Supertwin with original buddy-seat they found parked outside Bike Heaven, 123 Pier Street . . .'

'Too much detail,' I interrupted. 'And people don't do things "as one".' Anyway, I thought drawing was your thing. YOU are going to illustrate my books.'

There was an awkward silence for a bit.

'Verily,' Callum finally said, which sounded to me like a truce.

I suggested going on Aunt Laura's website to read her

Writer's Tips. I thought Callum might be more likely to take writing advice if it wasn't from me, and I think her Writer's Tips are better than her books, to be honest.

Aunt Laura's website has a nice picture of her smiling out of the screen at everybody. She looks quite glam for an Anciente Wrecke, and her blue eyes look sparkly and warm even on the computer.

There's nothing more discouraging, Aunt Laura's Writer's Tips begin, *than staring at a blank piece of paper or a blank screen and wondering where to start. How will that forbidding nothingness ever be filled with the wonderful magic of words, with the voices of characters you've conjured up with your own unique imagination, with the landscapes, journeys and adventures of your dreams?*

Callum and I let out a long sigh.

'There you see,' he said. 'We did that "as one".'

Aunt Laura's Writer's Tips went on. *Writing means using your imagination. It means making up things that don't really happen, to people who don't really exist. But you have to make your reader believe that they do happen, and the people are real. The inspiration to do that can only come from inside. From YOU. You can write about a fairy-tale adventure, or a pet you never had, even a journey to the moon. But to do it you have to think of how you felt in the best real adventure you can remember, how you felt about something or somebody you loved, how you felt on an exciting holiday to a strange new place. The details will be different and you can fill them in with your research. But your feelings can only come from you, and it's your feelings that will reach out to the reader, make them care about your story, and make them want to read on.*

'There you are, you see?' Callum said, flopping back on

my bed and puffing out his chest. 'I was expressing my feelings about the 1968 Harley Davidson Electraglide Supertwin.'

'Hmmm,' I said, scrolling down Aunt Laura's advice a bit faster and hoping for a clue. 'There's something wrong with that, but I'm not quite sure what. I wonder if maybe it's a boy/girl thing? Expressing feelings in different ways?'

Callum yawned and looked at his watch. 'Tell me tomorrow, Girl Writer,' he said, rolling off the bed. 'No, wait a minute, tell me Friday.'

'Why?'

'I start at Arlington tomorrow. Mum and Dad said it's going to be a very tiring time. You know, uniforms, getting used to a new laptop, enrolling in clubs and things, meeting all these posh new profs, reading lots of stuff. I don't know how I'm going to get through it.'

'Posh new profs? Don't they have teachers there?'

'Well, you know. Apparently lots of them have got "doctor" in front of their names. You got any of them at Falmer North?'

'I doubt it,' I said, opening my bedroom door. 'Do you want to go to the beach at the weekend?'

'Maybe,' Callum said. 'If I've got time. There's going to be a lot of homework.'

'It was a good idea, your bike thing,' I told him. 'Exciting.'

'Nah,' he said. 'You're the writer.'

'How's that thing about your dad?' I asked as we reached the front door.

'I don't know,' he said. But the look that flashed across his face told a different story.

'Come on, Clammy. You can tell me. I won't tell anyone.'

'I can't get my head together about it. I just want to forget anything's happening.'

'Look, if you tell me about it, we can stop it happening. You know? We can do ANYTHING together.'

That got a shadow of a smile, at least.

'I need to try to find out more, OK? Tell you Friday. By the pier at six-thirty?'

I nodded and he loped off looking dejected. Poor Callum. He's got enough on his mind, without starting a new school.

I lay awake, thinking about Callum's folks. Peter, his dad, has been like a favourite uncle to me. He used to push me and Callum on the swings at the big playground on the council estate when we were six. Candice never liked me going there, because it was 'rough'. But Peter didn't mind. Callum and I used to put on posh voices and pretend Peter was our butler. I hope those kids who were eight when I was six and who are probably all the hoodies and banshees at Falmer North can't remember the two pompous little brats who used to make fun of them then. I don't think I've changed very much . . . I still look about six . . . and I feel so different from all those other kids so I'm beginning to think maybe I'm still a pompous little brat.

But surely Peter and Andrea can't be splitting up, can they? They're always calling each other 'Bunny'. Do grown-ups who call each other 'Bunny' split up anyway? Is Peter calling his new girlfriend 'Bunny'? Don't they realise how miserable they're making Callum?

But enough of bunnies. It was all serious stuff that I couldn't do anything about at that moment, so how about a little escapism: the next fab bit of *The Lady of the Rings*, soon to be a movie starring Joaquin Phoenix as the Italian Stallion. To remind you, Lady C had decided that she would rather be a starving artist than forced into a squalide loveless marriage for mere millions.

The Lady of the Rings (ctd)

'I was born for better things, I was born to be an artist! I LIVE for my art. I will DIE for my art. Lothario, I must flee this place,' The Lady Cordelia beseeched imploringly, or implored beseechingly, of her servant. Pack my things and thongs - dresses, paints, easels and stuff (fill out details later, cut out thongs) also my costrel, buskins and bannock (Hah! Excellent olde wordes for water bottle, boots and bread) for I must flee immediately or else hurl myself to the savage rocks below.'

'Your Ladysheep, I will do your bidding forthwith,' gasped Lothario, his finely-modelled features besmirched by a grimace of pain at the thought of being parted from his Ladysheep, and her being dashed upon the rocks below.

Dear Reader, just to move things along, there's a bunch of stuff that happens next about Lothario's tragicke pleading with Lady C to stay put, and Lady C going on about how he's been her only friend apart from her beloved nanny, Nurse Ruby, and her old parrot. Her six squawking sisters and parents, however, have chained her to the Battlements of Despair, metaphorically speaking, because ... because ... well, that's the next exciting bit.

The Lady Cordelia looked deep into Lothario's eyes. 'They are making me marry a prince!' she cried.

'Wheeech prince, my Ladysheep?'

'ANY prince! I am to choose from six hundred! I am too young to marry! I need my space, my painting, my art! I must leave immediately, forthwith, pronto, now! For the first prince is e'en yet on the horizon.' And so saying, The Lady Cordelia threw open her trunks and began cramming them with dresses, shoes, jewels, paints and brushes since Lothario seemed too shocked to do it himself. (Lothario stands aghast now. I'm not sure whether you have to write anything else about somebody standing aghast or whether how someone looks aghast is obvious. I suppose it means having that look on your face people have when they've just seen the alien or the psycho with the chainsaw in horror films, though maybe that might be a bit much for this, since all Lady C's doing is packing her bags. The point is, she's never packed so much as a toothbrush in her life, so that's why he's aghast. It's all been down to him and the faithful nurse, Ruby, and the under-maid and the side-maid and the upstairs maid and the downstairs maid and the kitchen maid and the cupboard-under-the-stairs maid. Gadzooks! I wonder if they had a Loo Maid in those days? How embarrassing. Anyway, Lothario wonders why she is so desperately against her parents' plan and suspects she might have seen the Ominous Toades and the Black Swan of Deth. His aghastness is interrupted by ye doorbelle.)

Ding dong dell went the great, noble bell that hung like a vast ... (Note to reader: this is exactly the kind of problem writers have to struggle with all the time. How else can you describe the shape of a bell, except as a bell-shaped thing? Maybe think of something ominous here to set ye tone? Sack of serpents? A bat?) ... bat with folded wings.

The huge bell tolled its deadly ominous ring. Prince Kevin was at the great anciente oaken door that led from the anciente drawbridge that crossed the seething moat of foulle nauseating pukey vapours and slithering sea-serpents and weevil-wort.

(Dear Reader, if you're writing a Medieval Adventure, you have to have weird stuff like weevil-wort in. It's meant to show you that not only is the bleake world full of black knights, hooded executioners, enchanted forests, magicke mountains and mad, *firebreathing dragons, but even the plants are against you.)*

I wrote quite a lot about the next bit, in which the noble Prince Kevin turns up to plight his troth. I don't think this is as rude as it sounds – it's just a medieval way for a boy to tell a girl he fancies her, but nobly. 'Plight' means 'pledge' or 'promise' and 'troth' is 'truth' before anyone had spellcheck. I also wrote a lot of very tragicke heart-rending stuff about how old and decrepit Nurse Ruby is, and how long it takes her to get around the castle, what with twisting spiral stair-cases leading nowhere and shrieking, pooing bats and secret panels and hidden rooms full of skellingtons and vaste rattes and things. But it goes on for a bit and you get the idea. Anyway, after about nine years creaking about, Faithfulle Olde Nurse Ruby finally gets to Lady C's perfumed boudoir to tell her there's a bloke at the door, i.e. the noble Prince Kevin who has come to plight his troth.

'Prince Kevin is here to plight his troth.' The Lady Cordelia twisted the key in the heavy padlocks of her trunks, then thrust it between her maidenly bosoms before throwing her-self in a frenzy on to her embroidered duvet, uttering a hair-raising scream, which raised the hair on Lothario's head to reveal a finely-chiselled forehead. The Lady Cordelia briefly glimpsed this vision before swooning into a dead swoon in which she dreamed of scaling a finely-chiselled cliff. (There, surely that counts as a cliffhanger.)

Chapter Three

Ye Plotte Thickens

Laura Hunt's Top Tips for Budding Writers:
Whether you have a flair for describing
landscape, creating atmosphere, or
writing snappy dialogue, play to your strengths
and make the most them.

Erm, strengths. Long pause. I've got nice handwriting.
Must make sure book is printed as I wrote it, give it
authentic look. Wonder if I could have it printed
on parchment?

My worst fears are confirmed. After another day at Falmer North, I can confirm that the girls there only talk about one thing. Boys. Who is fit, who is buff, who is hench, who fancies who. The boys in my class are all mostly small, with squeaky voices, a bit like a herd of mice. Except for Snort (who grunts) and Tobylerone (OK, his name is Toby, but he has a very tiny, triangular head) who is about eight foot tall with a voice like a bear and said he is going to go out with

Buff Barbara by the end of this term. Tobylerone didn't say 'go out' with actually. If Candice could hear some of the language round there she would spontaneously combust.

Buff Barbara is a new girl in Year Eleven and you would have to be deaf and blind not to notice her from day one. She is like a very classy-looking cat. With make-up. And a miniskirt. And no fur. Actually, she doesn't look like a cat at all, but authors often say females are like felines. I wonder why that is? Maybe because girls are supposed to be catty. They are supposed to be bitchy, too, of course, but it's usually rude to say someone looks like a dog.

I have obviously got in with the wrong crowd. Well, I am not exactly 'in' but I kept my half full glass by fishing yesterday's shirt out of the laundry bin and wearing it all day today as if it was the coolest thing since iPods. Must admit it looked OK over my green velvet dress. I said the look was called 'retro chic' and told everyone I got the shirt in New York, that it cost a hundred and twenty-four dollars, and if they didn't believe me they could look in last month's *Elle*, which no one is going to be bothered to do, even if they could lift it up. So now I am one of the fashionista gang. How easy was that? So much for daring to be different though.

I have discovered the Mystery Girl with the long fair hair is called Viola. She sits in the quiet corner and reads all through breaktimes. She wears sandals. She looks troubled, as though there is an invisible grey cloud always drifting above her head.

I would like to talk to her, but the fashionistas say she is a nerd. They are very predictable and call her 'Viler' already. I suppose I am a nerd in fact. But I would prefer they don't find out.

So I am in a cleft stick.

I spent ages today looking for the writing competition on the Year Seven noticeboard but there was nothing. Maybe Candice invented it to make me feel better about going to Falmer North.

Am going to write all evening.

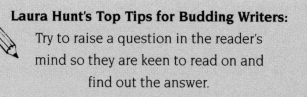

Laura Hunt's Top Tips for Budding Writers:
Try to raise a question in the reader's mind so they are keen to read on and find out the answer.

Something intriguing then, like, Lady Cordelia Arbuthnott shivered. The clock struck fourteen . . . ?

Ay *caramba*! I was getting into full flow when another distraction rendered my authorial voice distracted.

'CORDELIA!!!' yelled The Voice That Reduces Invincible Fortresses to Rubble. 'PHONE!!!'

I think it's time I got as serious about mobiles as everyone else is, though my battery is dead as usual.

'WHO IS IT???' I yelled down.

'DON'T KNOW!!!' came the reply, presumably deafening

for life whoever had taken the trouble to ring me up. It couldn't be Callum putting on a silly voice again. I bet he won't surface from his New Life for days yet, and when he does his New Life will probably be all he talks about.

I went downstairs. The receiver was lying forlornly abandoned next to the fish tank, and Blue was swimming forlornly abandoned about, hoping for something to happen like an exciting pair of glasses dropping in again. I MUST buy a friend for Blue, his life seems so lonesome.

'Hello?' I said, assuming there'd be a forlornly abandoned total silence by now.

'Hi,' said a voice. 'Is that Cordelia?'

'Verily,' said I, locked into Lady-Cordelia mode longer than I'd anticipated.

'It's Viola. I'm in your class. Um . . . you probably don't know who I am?'

'Oh. Yes, I do. Hi.'

'Sorry to bother you. My friend Minerva, from St Hilda's, had your number. Her mum knows your mum.'

'Oh. Right.'

'It's really stupid why I'm calling, you know? But Minerva told me your aunt is Laura Hunt. I couldn't believe it. She's been my favourite writer as long as I can remember. I didn't want to mention it at school. I thought they might laugh . . .'

'Yeah. They probably would,' I said.

'I don't want her autograph or anything like that. Well, it would be awesome to have it, of course, but . . . I just wondered if you'd have a minute to talk about her. It must be so amazing to have someone like that for an aunt. My aunt's a receptionist in an undertaker's.'

'I would think that's quite interesting,' I said, making conversation, not really aware of what I was saying. I was still rather surprised she'd called me up.

'It isn't. There's nobody to talk to.'

I couldn't figure out if Viola was joking or not. 'I've got some letters and things Aunt Laura's sent me,' I told her. 'Hardly any of it's secret or personal or anything. I could show you some of that if you like.'

There was such a long silence I thought Viola must have hung up or fainted. Then I heard a gulp. 'That . . . would be fantastic. Are you sure you don't mind?'

'No, it's cool. But I don't want to bring them to school.'

'Maybe I could come round?' Viola asked. I could hear how she was trying not to sound too keen. 'I only live round the corner.'

While I was waiting for Viola, I went back online and scrolled down Aunt Laura's website, hoping that maybe something interesting would pop up I could tell Viola about. No such luck. Same old stuff. School visit, a bit of writing, another school visit, tea with her daughter and the triplets, a picture of her cats, answers to fan mail. What is the point of being a Famous Writer if you never get to do Famous-like Things?

How does Aunt Laura write such successful books when all she does is sit with a cat or a triplet on her lap, and go round schools talking to kids?

I answered the door when the doorbell rang and led a timid- and dreamy-looking Viola upstairs. She gasped in awe at everything on her way to my room.

'Your house is *so* artistic. Are your parents artists?' she asked me.

I tried to suppress my laughter. 'Hell no. All this clutter is stuff from Mum's gallery. She's always buying the work of starving artists who can't sell it anywhere else. Sculptors, painters, mainly potters. It's why our teapots look like grand pianos or cabbages and we have forty fruit bowls for one mouldy apple.'

Viola would turn out to be the friend I've been looking for all my life. I was sure of it from the minute she flung herself on my bed and threw me a bumper box of rose and violet chocolates. I think these are the most expensive, and best, choccies in the world. Luckily most people think they taste like soap, so you don't have to share. It turned out that Viola wants to be a writer too. I asked if she'd heard anything about the alleged writing competition.

'No! Is there really one? That would be amazing.'

My heart sank. 'I guess if you haven't heard about it, it isn't true, then.'

'But we haven't had English yet; they're bound to mention it in English, aren't they?'

My heart dusted itself off and did a hopeful little hop, like one of those somersaulting toy puppies. I'm not sure I realised how much I cared about this till then.

'I really need this competition to get me to finish my

story,' I told her. 'The thing is, I find it so hard to write anything unless I have, like, a . . .'

'A goal? Something to aim for?' suggested Viola.

'Exactly! The trouble is, I want to write, but I find it really hard to get down to it.'

'I know what you mean. It's as though what you'd really like is to have *written* a book, and to see it there, gleaming with *your* name on it, sitting on a real shelf in a real bookshop,' said Viola, her grey eyes shining and her usually pale cheeks flushed. When she talked about writing, her shyness vanished and the little invisible cloud that floated over her head the rest of the time was just whisked away. 'But you don't want to actually have to do the hard bit, do you?' she continued. 'I feel like that too. But for me, writing is an escape. It isn't something I want to do, it's something I have to do.'

'But I do love the actual writing, too,' I added, anxious not to make her feel I was all mouth and no trousers. 'I mean, when I'm really getting on with The Lady of the Rings I get so excited that I forget everything else.'

'The Lady of the Rings? Is that what you're writing? Is it a comedy?'

'No. It's a romance! Why'd you think it was a comedy?'

'It's nothing,' she said hastily. 'Just . . . the title, you know, sort of seems like a parody.'

'Parody?' I blushed at the thought.

'Sorry, I thought, maybe, it was a send-up, like Bored of the Rings. Anyway, I'd love to read it. It's bound to be brilliant, because of your aunt.'

'But you see, I know you love Aunt Laura's stuff, and I do too, in a way. Or at least I used to. But I don't want to write like that. And I want to make my own name. Differently.'

'I do know what you mean. I don't want to be like anyone in my family either,' Viola said quietly. The cloud was back, only this time it was a full-on thunder cloud.

'Oh, I'm sure your family can't be that bad,' I said with a bright grin, trying to cheer her.

'You haven't heard anything about my folks have you? You know . . . from Snort, or anyone?' Viola asked anxiously.

'No. Why would I?'

'No reason. Stupid of me. It's just Tobylerone and Snort have got something against me . . .' Viola grimaced and hit herself on the head, rather too hard for a joke. 'Look, do you really have a pile of letters from Laura Hunt, or was that just a wind-up? I won't mind if you don't really.'

'Course I do. I've two great big box files full of e-mails I've written to her over the years, and all her replies,' I told her, fetching them. It's amazing, I haven't met Viola five minutes, and I'm telling her something I haven't told anybody else, not even Callum. 'I don't know why I kept it up. Even years ago I could see our e-mailing must be more interesting to me than to Aunt Laura. But I printed them all out because I like to read them for, well, inspiration and maybe for comfort. I suppose I just wanted someone to be out there, someone who knew how I felt . . .'

'I know what you mean,' Viola said. 'That's exactly how I feel too.'

'Here's one,' I said, handing it to her. 'It's an e-mail I wrote when I was eight.'

```
Dear Aunt Laura,
Please help. The princess is stuck in a
cave with her hands tied behind her back
and a bag of snakes over her head. The
water is rising. There is a prince on
the way but he has to kill off a thing
with lots of heads and every time he
cuts one off another one grows (a head,
I mean).
    Can you think of a way to free the
princess? I am a bit stuck.
    Love to Joan and Joan and the Three
Peas.
Cordelia xx
```

'Oh, she has two cats both called Joan,' I said, by way of explanation. 'You'd think she might've had a bit more imagination. And the Three Peas are her grandkids. Triplets. They weren't born then, they were just a very big fat pregnancy, so we called them the Three Peas, like peas in a pod. They're called the Three Bees now. Bessie, Bertie and Bobby.'

I thought Viola would laugh but instead she said, 'Great! You were so into writing even back then? What did she reply?'

'This,' I said, showing her Aunt Laura's short response.

Laura Hunt thanks you for your
marvellous message. Unfortunately she
has no time to personally answer all of
the many thousands of e-mails she
receives from all around the world.
With very best wishes for a Happy New
Year.

'It wasn't even New Year. It was March,' I told Viola. 'I cried buckets of course. Candice, that's my mum, must have rung Aunt Laura up about it, because I got this the next day.' I handed her another e-mail.

Darling Cordy,
Have just seen that awful e-mail - so
sorry about that. I had no idea my
website manager had put that ghastly
message on and have of course deleted it
and checked back. Luckily only thirty
fans got one and I've e-mailed to
apologise. But, darling, do let me know,
is the princess out of the cave? I think
it would be rather wonderful if she
freed herself, don't you? It would be
more modern than waiting for a prince!
Although, of course, I hope he defeats
the monster, perhaps by singing him to
sleep? Or hypnotising him to change his

ways and be a better monster and use his heads for good, rather than evil?

  Much love to all the family, purrs from Joan and Joan and gurgles from the Three Peas!!

Auntie Lol xxxx

Viola pored over this e-mail as if it was by Shakespeare or something.

'I can't believe I'm holding a letter that was actually written by Laura Hunt,' she said, breathily. 'I mean, not a letter to a fan, you know, but a real personal letter, to a member of her own family. And she is giving you advice! On how to write! You're so lucky!'

I was getting impatient. It was only a printed e-mail. What was so special about it?

'Yes, but looking back, is it good advice?' I said. 'I don't think Aunt Laura ever understood that kids love blood and guts and fighting. And it's romantic to be rescued by a prince! She's writing for a younger generation, and wants to teach everybody lessons all the time.'

'Hmmm. I'm not sure about all that,' said Viola. 'I think Laura Hunt writes about how I feel inside. I admit she's not Jane Austen, but she tells really good stories about what's happening now to people our age.'

'Yes, but the twenty-first century is so boring, and she's always writing about life issues, like we discuss in PSE. Friendship issues. Single parent issues – everyone in her books lives in dysfunctional families on grotty housing estates.'

'But that's how it is for . . . some people.' Viola's voice was a whisper, but her cloud loomed. 'Not everyone's as lucky as . . . as us.'

I suddenly realised I didn't know anything about Viola. And that then was not the right time to ask. She has one of those faces that have emotions scudding along just under her skin, like clouds in a windy October sky. What was her secret? I found myself drifting off as usual, imagining all kinds of exotic backgrounds for Viola. Maybe she was a princess disguised as a schoolgirl by her father, a king in some Nordic land afar, who had sent her to Falmer North to learn about the real world and choose a companion to accompany her back to her noble palace? And maybe that companion could be me?

'Verily,' I said. 'Thou hast ye nugget of truth twixt thy cherry lips.'

Viola laughed and begged to see some more of Aunt Laura's correspondence.

Well, I have got loads so I thought, why not?

It was almost as fun for me going through it as it was for Viola. It gave me a picture of all the things I've been trying to write for so long, almost like a portrait of myself as a writer, as well as of Aunt Laura. I also realised, looking through it all again, how important Aunt Laura is to me. She has always taken the time to listen and reply, even to my oddest of e-mails.

'Oh look, this one's a scream. I must have been about six when I wrote this,' I said to Viola, pulling out a battered piece of paper.

'You bet!' shrieked Viola, peering at it and giggling over my crazy spelling. 'How sweet, you really wanted to write a book about dogs, as if it was written BY dogs?'

'Yeah. It's quite funny really, I've got it somewhere here.'

I rummaged about and found my dog book. It was mainly big scrawly drawings in felt tip of dogs looking like their owners, but Viola didn't laugh or anything awful. 'Just like in *One Hundred and One Dalmatians*,' was what she did say.

'Yes. That's the trouble,' I replied. 'I sometimes think I'd like to write what Howard – my dad – calls a "novel of ideas". You know, a big clever grown-up book. But all my ideas seem to have come from something else that I've read or seen on telly or from films.'

'Don't worry about that,' said Viola. 'Apparently there are only seven different types of story in the world anyway. It's how you tell them that matters. Shakespeare didn't invent Romeo and Juliet. Well, he did invent *them*, but it was an old story of forbidden love that he retold.'

I'd never seen it like that before. Viola seemed to know a lot about this sort of thing.

She read every letter in the file I'd given her and kept praising me and Aunt Laura. It gave me a warm soft glow, like being around a kind twin sister. But Viola sighed as she closed the file. 'I don't think you realise how amazing this is. It's like a series of writing lessons, but it's also a picture of you.'

'That's just what I was thinking,' I told her.

'Are you still writing to her? This all seems to be up till you were ten years old.'

'Yeah, there's a whole other file of e-mails, loads of them. And, well, I was just about to post this . . . I've been writing more proper letters recently, partly to practise my handwriting, because I think authors need to have good handwriting for all the book signings they do and partly because when I do that she sometimes writes a proper letter back, and it's nice to keep.'

I showed Viola the letter that was on my desk.

Dear Aunt Laura,

I hope you appreciate my violet ink and cream vellum notepaper. I think I read that Philip Pullman has learned calligraphy, so I thought it might make me also a good writer. I've started at my new school and Candice is in mourning. She wishes she could afford to send me to St Hilda's so I could be a nice, well-behaved girl in a uniform and fulfill my natural inborn genius. Howard says it's all an unfair system that will come crashing down when the revolution comes.

I need your advice. I am getting on very well with my new romance, The Lady of the Rings. It is to be the first of a trilogy, or maybe a quartet. I'm already planning the film version. I don't want too many computer graphics in it – the Enchanted Forest and the monsters in the moat should be proper animated models as it is more atmospheric.

Who do you think should do the film? Ang Lee? Peter
Jackson? Stephen Spielberg? I am not sure he is quite
intellectual enough for me, although I do think he is very
good at mass appeal, as you are. But I have been wondering
about my name.

'Oh, you don't need to see this bit,' I said, suddenly embarrassed.

But Viola did want to see it. 'Oh please,' she said. 'I won't
laugh, I promise.'

I relented.

Cordelia Lucinda Arbuthnott seems too long for the front
cover of a book. Also, I would want it to be embossed in gold
or silver (or possibly silvery pink, although, with no
disrespect to your own lovely covers, I do think the colour is a
trifle overdone and so obviously girly). Should I change my
name or have a pen name? Or what if I just use my initials,
like JK Rowling? Is that why she used just her initials do you
think? Or is it true that her publishers didn't think boys
would read a book by a woman? I think CL Arbuthnott
looks quite good, but it reads as Clarbuthnott, which sounds
a bit crabby, doesn't it?

I am really worried about this, so please do reply.

I've made the enclosed two collars for Joan and Joan. The
bells will warn passing birdies that they are coming.
Lots of love,
Cordelia xx

'Do you think I should send it?'

'Of course! Anyway, Cordelia Arbuthnott is a . . . really distinctive name,' said Viola.

'Viola Larpent is much better, and puts you right on the middle shelf in bookshops. I wish my name didn't begin with an "A"; it'll be so high up on the shelves.'

Viola looked sympathetic.

'Maybe you should ask her about that,' she said. 'I'm sure names are important.'

Then suddenly we both jumped about a mile into the air as a crashing sound came from the kitchen, followed by very raised voices. I could feel my cheeks go more fuschia than Lady Cordelia's.

I don't believe that my parents would choose the time I have a new friend round to have an almighty row.

Viola's cloud returned. She shrank into my duvet and muttered something about how she'd better be going because she'd just remembered an urgent dental appointment. It was seven-thirty.

'Don't be daft. And don't worry,' I said. 'Howard's just probably smashed one of Candice's precious pots. Let's investigate.'

We went down to the hall. Viola put on her anxious-vole look and disappeared behind her hair as we passed the kitchen, where Howard and Candice seemed to be having some sort of Big Discussion. Viola looked round at me, as if whatever was happening was all her fault. I put my finger to my lips.

'Don't worry,' I said. 'We're writers. It's research.'

Viola looked shocked, but I grabbed her arm and she stayed put. She even grinned a bit, as if she was doing something naughty but fun, and that didn't usually happen to her.

'I don't know what you mean, "it's not going to be easy",' Howard was saying.

Candice made some groaning, anguished noises.

'Look, if we can't do this for Peter,' Howard went on, 'who can we do it for?'

'Why doesn't he just use a hotel?' Candice hissed.

'He thinks they're tacky for something like this,' Howard said. 'I've never known him act this way before – he's going on about how wonderful love is, wanting to celebrate it . . . But subterfuge isn't Peter's thing. It'll be more relaxing for him if it's somewhere familiar – and of course if it's here, there's no chance of Andrea getting suspicious. We mustn't let Cordelia in on it of course. She'd never be able to keep it from Callum. And naturally Peter is determined that Callum shouldn't find out – he's worried he'd tell Andrea and ruin everything.'

'I can understand that, but what about Barbara?' I heard Candice ask. 'She's at Cordelia's new school, for God's sake. She might let the cat out of the bag.'

'She won't,' Howard said. 'More than her life's worth.'

Viola and I waited outside with bated breath. I heard Howard groan. 'Andrea'll kill us when this farcical affair all comes out,' he said.

I clutched Viola for support. But I could see the penny hadn't dropped. I pulled her down the hall to the front door.

'What's going on?' Viola whispered, mystified.

'It's terrible,' I hissed at her. 'They're talking about their best friends, Peter and Andrea. They're my best friend Callum's parents. My own parents are plotting some kind of terrible betrayal. I can't believe they'd help Callum's dad do something against his mum – doesn't friendship count for anything these days? What *can* it mean but one thing? All that stuff about hotels – and keeping the affair from Andrea – who is Peter's WIFE and Callum's MUM?'

'Callum's dad is doing it with somebody else?' Viola asked.

'Of course he is. Callum's suspected it for a while and now we have proof.'

'Well, worse things happen,' said Viola, and I caught a look in her eye fleetingly that wasn't pain or anger quite, but a mix of both.

'But this is terrible. How can my horrible parents be helping him be so nasty?'

'They said Barbara might let the cat out of the bag at school – isn't she that girl who looks like a supermodel? Can she be the one they were talking about?'

'She can't be,' I said. 'She's only sixteen and Peter's about nine hundred. He's got a fat belly and he's losing his hair. Maybe one of our teachers is called Barbara. But whoever it is, I'm going to find out.'

There was a sudden hush. Had my folks heard us? We scampered upstairs and made a big show of coming down again, very noisily.

'CORDELIA! Is that you?' came The Voice That Moves Mountains.

'You'll have to go,' I whispered to Viola. 'Don't say a word to anyone about this. But we'll have to stop it somehow. Poor Callum. And his poor mum. We have to help them out.'

'I'm with you,' Viola said. 'Like you said about research – it'll make a great story.'

'It's not a story,' I said as she went out into the night. 'This is for real.'

I hardly slept because I kept wondering who the mystery Barbara was. Not Mrs Warren, surely? Unless Peter is taking this Bunny thing further than I thought. Still, Dear Reader, instead of getting you all sleepless too, I'll share the next instalment of The Greatest Novel Ever Written. Remember Prince Kevin is downstairs and The Lady Cordelia has just fallen into a swoon.

The Lady of the Rings (ctd)

In a great, big, blinding flash of wisdom, Lothario had a huge light bulb of an idea. He would dress up as The Lady Cordelia and refuse the prince on her behalf! Then his beloved Ladysheep would not have to leave her castle but could stay forever painting her pretty paintings in the shelter of the great, noble, vaulted, *mullioned, turreted walls and they could live happily ever after forever as Noble Lady and Faithful and Devoted Manservant.*

Here's a little summary to get you over the next bit of my enthralling medieval tale, Dear Reader, as it's quite long, but rest assured, in the full version, my amazing literary talents and Gifte for Bringing a Bygonne Age to Life do full justice to Lady C's haunted and tragicke life.

Basically, Prince Kevin is standing, nervously holding his crown in one hand and anxiously clasping a gold ring in the other, with which he hopes to plight his troth.

Faithful retainers (which means grovelling servants) appear from every nook and cranny, gossiping respectfully, saying, 'Isn't he handsome? Isn't he faire? His sparkling eyes! His wavy haire! His silken cloak beyond compare!' They were very much looking forward to the wedding banquet where, by anciente customme, they would all get a slice of meate and of bannock, instead of the usual stale, olden gnawed entrails and hunks of pig's bladder they usually got. The rumour was, they would also get a thimbleful of asti-spumante, which was almost like ye champagne, and which, they had been told, tasted quite different from their ration of moate water – which was all they usually got, although the baby servants were given badger's milk every second Thursdaye.

Prince Kevin was rehearsing his chat-up lines in his head. 'I must not make the joke about swimming the moat so she can see my breast stroke. I must not ask her if she's seen any good disembowelments lately. I must not admire her shapely wimple ...'

Well, you get the idea. By the way, I am not tempting Ye Youthe Of Ye Nation into Eville Foulle Thoughts or anything – a wimple is a kind of hatte, and I'm sure they were often shapely, if you liked that sort of Thingge.

Noble Lothario then has a problem dressing up as her Ladysheep, because Lady C has locked up her trunks (that's big boxes) with chaines and padlockes, etc, and he has to smash his way into them, in a passionate, masculine way in order to get access to her lacy, feminine garments, etc. I realise that dressing up as a woman does not necessarily seem like a heroic male activity, and may even make Lothario seem like a bit of a wuss, but one thing I've learned about writing is that the next thing that seems about to happen isn't necessarily what you think it's going to be.

So Ye Booke goes on like this:

The padlock burst asunder, the lid flew open and AAAAAAAAAARRRRRRRGHHHHH!

(Note to reader: this is a different kind of cliffhanger to the one before.)

Chapter Four

Ye Writing Competition, Calloo Callay

Laura Hunt's Top Tips for Budding Writers:

If you want to be a writer: Read lots . . .

Yes, but does it matter what? Today, I have read the entire cornflakes box, plus ingredients of Xerxes's food, because I am convinced that new Luxurious Purr ('Puts a shine on their fur/ Happy cats prefer Purr') will be healthier for him than Kat Kit, which Candice buys in bulk because it's cheaper. Kat Kit instead of Purr. Falmer North instead of St Hilda's. That's life in the Arbuthnott household.

'CORDELIA!!!!!'

There she goes again, interrupting ye traine of my thought. I'm sure Candice's caterwauling must be bad for the house – start the walls cracking or something. It's certainly bad for the inmates. Little does she know I have stumbled on her Horrible Plan for helping Peter in his betrayal of her oldest friend.

'IT'S TWENTY PAST EIGHT! TIME YOU WERE OFF TO SCHOOL!!!'

I stuffed The Greatest Novel Ever Written back in my sock drawer. I think it's coming along really well, although I say it myself. Maybe I'll show it to Viola. She's already my Number One fan.

I grabbed my bag and raced downstairs, stepping on the tail of lazy Xerxes, slowest-moving cat in feline history. He hissed at me, looked offended and sloped off to comfort himself with food – even if it is only Kat Kit – and threw his usual yearning look at the forlorn and lonesome Blue. (Do cats ever eat goldfish in real life? I hope it is only in cartoons.) I think he is offended because Candice has recently given him a food bowl shaped like a poodle with GOOD DOG painted on the side.

Speaking of food, Candice had forgotten to do my packed lunch as usual. When I pointed this out, she started the usual speech about how busy she is slaving away at the gallery 'encouraging young artists'. And plotting the ruin of a young life, I nearly said. Howard had his head in an anciente medieval text book but waved a hand limply without looking up. Anyone would think they were not planning the disembowelment of all Callum's happiness and the truncation of his youthe and joye.

Couldn't resist a parting shot to swell her guilt. 'Don't worry about lunch,' I called out as I left. 'I'll just get fashionably scrawny. Byee!!'

I was out of the door and halfway down the road while Candice was scrambling in her bag for lunch money. Hah! Let her suffer.

I was actually looking forward to school today. Well, almost. It was our first English lesson, with a proper old-fashioned English teacher, Mrs Parsing. Even hoodies and banshees refer to her as Eight-Brains Parsing, which is a good omen. Surely Viola will be right and she will announce the story competition today, won't she?

English was in fact the first lesson of the day. Mrs Parsing is about nine foot tall with a voice like a foghorn, tiny glasses, nice, grey, tight-curled hair and wears proper, long skirts and matching jackets. A real Old Skool teacher. She doesn't try to cuddle up to the students and be their friend like Miss Hardy, the RE teacher who wears the Star of David in one ear, the crescent of Islam in the other and a crucifix round her neck. Miss Hardy was wearing a T-shirt yesterday with the atheist's prayer on it: *Oh God, if there is a God, save my soul, if I have one.* I like that prayer because Howard has it up in his study and of course Miss Hardy is trying to be all things to all people, which is nice. But I have seen her SMOKING only just outside the school gates which is a disgusting example for the whole school. I was going to report her but Viola said it was a snotty thing to do and I should be more tolerant. I froze at a sudden throught. Could Miss Hardy be the dread Barbara?

Viola had saved me a seat at the front and I really wanted to sit right up close to Mrs Parsing so I could look eager and keen and talented without anyone noticing. But I hung back for a minute because I didn't want to look nerdy. Viola waved at me and I could hear Zandra and Jolene giggling. I was sure I could hear the words 'nerdy swot', but I thought, What would Jesus do? which is a strange thought for someone in an atheist household but quite useful on occasions. And the answer came to me quickly. Jesus would definitely push past the sheep and sit with the swine, or something like that. So I stuck my tongue out at Jolene and plonked myself down next to Viola. She looked so happy I nearly hugged her and then I realised I had just beaten Tobylerone to the seat.

The weird thing is, everyone enjoyed Mrs Parsing's lesson. Even Snort and Tobylerone stopped messing around and Zandra, Jolene, Sharon, Karen and Lauren didn't text each other once. It's strange they do it at all really, since they always sit together. Mrs Parsing gave us a brilliant talk on poetry and, unbelievably, I forgot all about the story competition until Viola nudged me and pointed to the clock with a look of anguish. Help. It was almost the end of the lesson and she hadn't mentioned it! Viola pleaded with her eyes and mouthed 'Ask'. So I did.

'Thank you for reminding me, Cordelia. I had almost lost track of the time,' said Mrs Parsing. She really is one of those excellent teachers who can memorise all the Year Seven names in week one. How do they do it? 'There are, thanks to the generosity of a parent, book tokens for the winners of our Year Seven Short Story Competition. The school magazine will publish a selection of entries and we are hoping that maybe even the local paper will also support us by publishing the winners in each category. This is a wonderful opportunity for you all to practise your writing in a way that you will really enjoy.'

Mrs Parsing then announced the categories – romance, comedy and thriller – and went on to explain them. 'A romance does not have to be a traditional boy meets girl story. It could be boy and boy,' (snorts from Snort) 'or girl and girl,' (squeals from the banshees and Viola went bright red and looked at her shoes, which are old-fashioned sandals, which I would like to wear too and make me feel very fond of her) 'or, perhaps more interestingly, the romance of a place you have visited in some distant far-flung land,' boomed Mrs Parsing. 'And the thriller doesn't have to be in the typical Hollywood style, it could be any thrilling experience – the birth of a baby sister for instance,' she peered over her specs at the hoodies, who all groaned. 'Though of course if we have any budding Ian Flemings in our midst, we will all be thrilled.'

'Who's Ian Fleming, Miss?'

'He wrote James Bond,' Mrs Parsing informed us.

'Nah, that was Sean Connery.'

'Nah. Cubby Broccoli.'

Mrs Parsing looked beady. 'Like many marvellous films,' she said, cutting into the growing conversation, 'the Bond series originated as books. The magic of books translates wonderfully into cinema and, who knows, maybe a story by one of you will one day be among them.'

I could barely listen for excitement. *The Lady of the Rings* directed by Peter Jackson. With computer graphics by Callum Carstairs. Nominated for twelve Oscars . . . Now that I know the competition is really happening, I reckon if I work really hard I could have a go at all three categories. They've got to be between two and five thousand words each and I've already written about two thousand words of *The Lady of the Rings*. I will enter it in romance, obviously.

Viola and I linked arms after the lesson and bounced down the corridor singing.

'You'll win it, no probs,' Viola said.

'You should do one too,' I said. 'I won't mind if you win.'

'But I'll mind,' Viola told me. 'It's you that really deserves it.'

Viola is really very nice. If anyone else said that I'd think, Yeeech, or, She's lying. But she does always seem to be more interested in other people than herself.

When I got home, everybody was out, except lazy Xerxes, who hissed at me again to let me know he hadn't forgotten about the tail incident. I don't think it's natural for a cat to be indoors so much – he's becoming a couch potato. He'd have the telly on if Howard didn't keep forgetting to change the dead battery in the remote.

I ran upstairs, pulled The Greatest Novel Ever Written out of the sock drawer, and looked at it anew as the winning romance entry in the writing competition that will make me a star.

I was just rehearsing my acceptance speech ('Thanks so much for this honour, but there are far more deserving winners than me, this is just a little something I dashed off in an evening . . .') when the doorbell rang. I went reluctantly downstairs. Lazy Xerxes hissed, but looked bored with the whole business now, and I found Callum standing on the doorstep. I hardly recognised him at first; he seemed to have turned into an adult in two days. He looked about fifty, was wearing a horrible bottle-green blazer and a clean white shirt and a tie! All knotted straight. Worse, he had brushed his hair.

'Hello,' I said. 'I thought you weren't going to be free until the weekend.'

'Yeah,' Callum replied. 'Well, I was passing.'

That's not true, I thought to myself. He takes the school bus now, which drops him at the corner of his road. I asked him how it was all going and he said terrific.

'We've all got laptops and there's a swimming pool. How about you?'

'Great.'

He went on about Doctor this and Doctor that and how they're all going on an art trip to Italy and the art teacher told him he was 'exceptionally talented'. Just because he can draw a bit, Callum thinks he's going to be the next Leonardo da Vinci.

'Do you want to come in?' I asked.

'No,' he said unexpectedly. 'Are you doing anything right now?'

'Well . . . I was just . . .'

'Great. Come on.' He was off down the road before I

could draw breath. I almost shut lazy old flea-bitten Xerxes's head in the door in my hurry to leave. Our relationship is definitely going through a bad patch.

'I haven't fed him yet! Supposing he snaffles Blue,' I panted, catching up with him.

'Who?'

'Xerxes. Anyway, where are we going?'

'You know that stuff I was telling you about my dad?' Callum asked.

'Um,' I said, thinking of the conversation I'd overheard between Howard and Candice. How could I tell Callum about that? Even if your parents are doing something wrong, they're still your parents. I felt that I wanted to face them myself about it before I started telling people, even Callum.

'Well, I think I'm on to something,' Callum went on. 'I just heard Dad making a lot of secret calls on his mobile, whispering and all that, stopping talking if I got anywhere near him. But I think I heard him arrange to meet someone at six o'clock at The Castle. It's that bar with turrets and stuff at the top of the high street. It's ten to six now – if we hurry we might get there at the same time.'

'But we can't just walk in there,' I said. 'You have to be with a grown-up.'

'Maybe we can find a spare one,' he replied.

I couldn't believe it. 'Are you kidding?' I said in amazement. 'Ask a complete stranger to take two eleven-year-olds into a bar with them? Did your parents never tell you anything about how weird some grown-ups are?'

'Well, anyway,' Callum said. 'Maybe we can just hang about there and see what happens.'

We arrived at The Castle just before six. It's so different from the castles I'm always imagining – like Lady C's castle in The Greatest Novel Ever Written. There's no moat, for a start. There is a drawbridge, but it doesn't draw – it's just a few bits of wood and a chain or two stuck on the pavement. Even the two flaming torches by the door are fake – just flickering electric bulbs when you look at them closely. There was no sign of Callum's dad. We crept round the building, looking in the brightly-lit windows. A few bored people were sitting around staring into their drinks. There was a girl, with legs like a giraffe and long blond hair down to her miniskirt, standing at the bar with her back to us and chatting to a George Clooney look-alike. Well, it can't be her, I thought, she looks too young to be in a bar, never mind anything to do with poltroon Pete.

Suddenly, Callum gripped my arm. 'There he is! Look!'

Behind us, Callum's dad, swag-bellied poltroon Pete himself was crossing the fake drawbridge, going through the fake olde archway, and then we could see him through the window crossing over to the bar . . . and . . . and . . . going over to the girl in the miniskirt!

They threw themselves into each other's arms! They kissed! Yeecch! George Clooney look-alike patted them both on the back, gave Callum's dad a piece of paper (was that money?!) and rushed off looking at his watch.

I've never seen Callum's eyes go so round.

'Do you know who they are?' I whispered to him.

'No idea,' he just managed to say.

'Impertinent, hedge-born harpy,' I snarled, but he gave no flicker of a smile.

Poltroon Pete and Harpy were laughing. How could they? They obviously weren't giving a thought to Peter's poor wife Andrea and his only son, Callum.

We hung about outside trying to get a better view, but people kept getting in the way. Then we saw the girl properly for the first time and I am still in shock. I couldn't believe it. How much more could a human being stand? We were witnessing something at that moment that even I, as a soon-to-be-award-winning Author and Creative Person Who Can Imagine Anything Imaginable, should not have to see. Because the miniskirted harpy was Buff Barbara. Suddenly Callum's cosy dad and a girl from my school, the dread Buff Babs herself, were in each other's arms again.

Is it worth growing up, if it turns out like this?

Revolting Barbara and Baldicoot Peter then turned and headed for the exit arm in arm. What had happened to the old fat geezer I used to love? We snapped into action. Callum and I hammered round the corner of The Castle as his dad came out of the fake entrance and – horrors! – flagged down a cab. We were standing on the street corner jumping up and down with anger as the cab set off with our treacherous target in it, when a car that looked like it had been written off in a car crash came round the corner. And who should be leaning out of the back window but

Tobylerone! He saw us standing there and the car came screeching to a stop in front of us.

'Need a ride?' came the bear-like growl of Tobylerone.

'FOLLOW THAT CAB!' Callum and I shouted at him. It's so wonderful when life is Just Like A Film.

Tobylerone threw open the back door and we chucked ourselves in. Hearing the constant, panic-stricken voices of Howard and Candice when talking about cars, we searched for the seat belts and miraculously found some. In the front was Snort, and at the wheel was a thick-necked boy I didn't know.

'My big brother,' Toby said, seeing me staring.

'Hi,' said his big brother, not looking round. 'You're Fizzy Oake's little girl's mate, aren't you?'

'Shut it,' growled Tobylerone.

'I don't know what you mean,' I said, puzzled.

'You will, sunshine, you will,' Toby's big brother said.

There was a loud crunching and crashing noise, and the car shuddered a lot.

'Haven't had this car long,' Toby's big brother explained, as the car then shot off.

'Is that a blazer you're wearing?' Snort suddenly asked Callum.

'Er . . . yes.'

'It's cool. I like the colours,' Snort said. He stared at Callum closely. 'How d'you make your ears do that?'

We could still see the cab up ahead. Toby's big brother put his foot down. The cab stopped for a traffic light. So did we, but unfortunately did it by crashing straight into the back of the cab. Toby's big brother said a few words I will not repeat until we get to *Girl Writer Volume IV*, which hopefully will be for an age group that can listen to such language without needing to be sent to a special Men In Black brain-washing school where they can erase your memory.

Everyone was OK and we all piled out on to the street. Callum and I ducked behind the car to watch as treacherous, oafen Peter gave his swearing cab driver what looked like a great deal of paper money.

'Keep the change,' I heard him say. 'I'm in a bit of a hurry.'

The cab driver came round the back of his cab to check the damage, counting Peter's money at the same time. He said a few more words that you would all recognise but which I can't repeat here and Toby's brother said a few back. Toby went all embarrassed and said they should swap car numbers, when I realised Peter and Buff Babs had disappeared into the crowd.

'Follow that dad,' Callum hissed at me, and we hurried off.

We hurtled down a scary-looking alleyway and saw Callum's dad and Buff Barbara turning a corner in the distance. 'Are you sure this is a good idea?' I gasped.

'No, I don't think I do any more,' said Callum slowly. 'You know, you can know someone all your life . . .' he whispered. He had stopped dead in the alleyway and was looking as if he was about to be sick, which was how I was feeling too. ' . . . but you don't really know them at all.'

'Funny you should say that,' I said to Callum. 'There's something I've been meaning to mention . . .' I knew I had to tell him that my folks were in on the plot.

'Stop it,' he said before I could say a word more. 'I don't want to see or hear anything else. I can't handle this.'

'Neither can I,' I agreed, chickening out. 'I think it's time we went home.'

I'll let you all recover from the horrible revelations above by showing you the next bit of my book. I don't know if the older generation are having a bad influence, but, phew, The Greatest Novel Ever Written was getting pretty hot. Maybe it'll be the first book to get an 18-certificate. Check this out (Lothario has just smashed the padlock and screamed):

The Lady of the Rings (ctd)

The padlock burst asunder, the lid flew open and AAAAAAAAAARRRRRRGHHHHH!

Lothario looked around in darkest despair, his bellow waking the very dead from their mulchy graves (but fortunately not Lady Cordelia out of her swoon). For the Lady Cordelia's tubes of oile paint had squeezed themselves all over her beautiful silken and velveten and erminen and satin garments. How many times had he flitted, silent as an ant in moccasins, when she was having a snooze/taking forty winks/kipping/slumbering, around her boudoir screwing the lids of her paint tubes on? And how could he make Prince Kevin believe he *was really the lovely Lady C if he looked as if he had just spent the afternoon doing a bit of decorating?*

There was only one thinge unspoiled to wear – the emerald velvet dress as worn, to whit, verily, by The Lady C as she lay swooning a deep swoon.

Dear Reader, this is where it all gets a bit tricky, and you may want to put your hands over your eyes. Lothario has got to undress The Lady C without her waking up, and without being discovered by the Earl and Earless Arbuthnott (Note to self: must look up what a lady earl is called) who would surely get hold of Ye Wronge End of Ye Twigge and have him hung, drawn and quartered, denounced as a rank, lily-livered, pox-hearted remnant, have his head and other bits stuck on a pole outside the castle, and then flog him within an inch of his life.

They didn't mess about in those days when it came to revenge.

So Lothario bars the door and with trembling fingers, unbuttons the two thousand tiny pearls that hold The Lady C's gown together. But it's all OK, because the stuff girls wore under their outer clothes in those days was so complicated that The Lady C was still wearing almost as much when Lothario had finished than before he began.

I wrote this as a very Dramatique Scene in which The Lady Cordelia nearly wakes up or Lothario's nearly discovered about a million times, which I know you will find keeps you on the edge of your seat, Dear Reader, when you come to read the Fulle Booke when it is piled high in bookshops the length and breadth of the Kingdom (should that be Queendom?).

Anyway, Lothario puts Lady C's kit on and crashes off downstairs, falling over her long skirts and uttering incomprehensible medieval curses. Eventually he gets to the door, and the Greate Booke continues like this:

'Faugh! Who is this vision that descends the stairs?' cried Prince Kevin in alarm, on spotting a tall figure swathed in emerald velvet descending the winding staircase. The arms of the figure were, as Prince Kevin could not help noticing, covered in thick, dark hairs. His wise old father, King Nigel of Nordor, had told him The Lady Cordelia was blessed with the gracefulle limbs of a racehorse. The approaching figure, Prince Kevin thought, was built more like a carthorse, or even a cart.

Prince Kevin was in a Fogge of Indecision. He would much rather have been jousting, or adding a state-of-the-arte ferret-hurler to his chariot, or playing his favourite game of snooker with cannonballs, than wooing a hairy-armed maiden, but his father had told him to get his acte together before he was sent off to fight in foreign lands where his vital royal parts might be damaged in ye cutte and thruste of battle. So he tried his best.

'Thou art a vision of loveliness like what I have

never seen, gadzooks,' babbled Kevin, throwing himself to ye floor in what he hoped looked like devotion, and realising he had forgotten to remove his iron jousting elbow-guards before coming out.

'Hell's bells,' quoth the noble Prince with a squeal. 'Elbows of a thousand buffoons!'

'Oh you don't like my elbows, do you?' quoth the outraged Lothario from the staircase. 'Begone thou reeking, dog-hearted hempseed! Thou mildewed manikin!' Lothario squeaked indignantly, stamping his feet in what he hoped was a maidenly fashion. 'I have never been so insulted in my life!' He turned to the mountainous horde of faithful retainers lurking in the shadows of the shadowy vaulted chamber and cried in a shrill, squealing tone that reminded Prince Kevin of the sound of the rack giving his faithful manservant his weekly stretching. 'This oaf said I had the elbows of a buffoon! No, a thousand buffoons! Throw him to the wolves! No, on second thought,' he added, because he was a kindly soul and wished poor Prince Kevin no harm, 'show him the door. Then show him Ye Boote in Ye Bumme.'

'No worries,' Prince Kevin said. 'I'm out of here.' (Note to self: think of something more princely later.)

And so saying, ye Gloomy Knight pocketed back his ring, drew his cloak about him and vanished into ye gloomy night.

Lothario sped up the enormous staircase, up and up,

four steps at a time. Even the dimme olde watchful eyes of Faithfulle Nurse Ruby realised The Lady Cordelia had never done such a thing before. Slowly, slowly, like a great ocean liner turning in the midst of a narrow canal, the old retainer turned to hobble, shamble, dodder, stumble and lurch after her beloved Ladyship. If it was her Ladyship ...

Meanwhile, high above, Lothario returned to The Lady Cordelia's boudoir. There she lay, in her maidenly whale-bone corsetry, still sprawled atop her richly embroidered duvet.

Chapter Five

Hatching Ye Planne

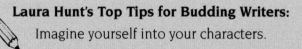
In fact, it is hard to concentrate on my Great Romance because I cannot get the foul image of swag-bellied Pete kissing Buff Babs out of my head. My mind feels all clogged up, as though I'm in a horrible swamp. I have realised that suspecting it is one thing and witnessing it is quite another. Poor, poor Callum. What must he be feeling now? It's the kind of thing you read about in newspapers – dirty old men dating schoolgirls. You don't expect it to happen to you.

Sigh. If only life were like my great novel, full of dreamy ladies with beauteous souls, faithful nurses, princes on steeds of fire and all that – instead of Callum's seedy old dad slobbering over people in bars and my seedy old parents helping him.

It's a shame this has made me see my parents so differently. I've always loved Howard so much mainly because he seemed so old-fashioned, like frayed old books and comfy cushions – now he doesn't seem so cosy after all. Candice has never been cosy exactly (it's hard to be cosy when you're worried all the time over things like me failing the scholarship exam for Barnaby High and why you can't afford the ten tutors all the other children had) but she's always been good-hearted, or so I've thought until now.

How quickly things can change.

Checked e-mails before going to bed. Not that there usually are any. But, gadzooks, there were two – one from Callum, one from Aunt Laura.

Callum's one said (I've had to correct the spelling here because otherwise posterity will not have a hope of reading what will obviously be an important document once I have become a world-famous author):

```
Can't sleep. Keep thinking of Dad. Are
you still up? We must do something. Will
you help? Do you think all this will
turn me into a psychopath?
   Farewell. Your servant till hell
freezeth over. C.
```

I quickly wrote a reply:

Don't worry. Everything will be fine.
Trust me, we'll think of a plan. You
will not become any more of a psychopath
than you are now.

Farewell. Your friend till the very
heavens cracketh and raineth burning
locusts across the land. C.

Aunt Laura's message said:

Darling Cordy,
Thanks for your gorgeous letter, I LOVE
your pen! Is it a fountain pen with real
purple ink? I hope you are not getting
too grown up to do me any drawings
though. I miss your little doodles, I
think they are brilliant!

I wouldn't worry too much about your
name. It is a very nice name, but it is
the book that counts. Having said that,
did you know that Lucy Daniels, who wrote
'The Animal Ark' series, is a made-up
name? The publishers decided 'D' would be
a good initial and would be close to some
other famous writer - it might have been
Roald Dahl - on the shelves, so maybe you
have a point! Lucy Daniels in fact isn't
one person at all, but lots of different

people all writing under one name!

I agree that Peter Jackson would be a great director for your romance, but don't be too disappointed if it takes a little while to sell the film rights; there's such a lot of competition. But I'm sure you will!!! I would LOVE him to direct *Orphan Jenny* or *Mad Bad Dad*. My agent is in touch with his people but these things take time.

Joan ADORES her collar. But Joan got cross with hers! I had to take the bells off – the constant tinkling tried the nerves after a while. I hope you don't mind. Are you coming to stay any time soon? It's been ages since your last visit.

Bessie, Bertie and Bobby have been here for a week. They are SO adorable, but goodness, I need to get my head down to some hard writing now!

Big kisses to Howard and Candice.

And loads of love to you and Blue and Xerxes.

Lolly xxxxxxxxxx

That CAN'T be true about Lucy Daniels can it? I LOVED those books. But it goes to prove my point that names can be important. Cordelia Daniels is rather dashing. Or maybe Cordelia Dickens . . . Dickens is a tried and trusted brand. If I put C. Dickens a few people might pick it up thinking it was The Great Charles.

I typed my name, c-o-r-d-e-l-i-a a-r-b-u-t-h-n-o-t-t , into an anagram generator thingy on the Net. It came up with 'hot drab ulceration'. This was depressing for a moment, till I realised I must have missed out a 'T' when I typed it in. But the word author does shine out of <u>Arbuthno</u>tt! Amazing! I played around on the anagram website instead of going to bed. I added my middle name, Lucinda, which gave me an anagram of 'ridiculed blatant con author'. Hmm. But wait a minute, 'Lothario' is in my anagramed name too! Err . . . Cordelia Arbuthnott makes 'Lothario, butt dancer'.

Does this mean Lothario really works in a medieval lappe-dancing clubbe and is in fact a traitor to her Lady-sheep? Are all grown-ups traitors really?

This is how we authors must work, endlessly playing with words until The Truth shines blindingly through. It is a hard life. I think I am getting writer's block.

Laura Hunt's Top Tips for Budding Writers:

Writer's block? Think of ordinary objects:
an apple, a cat, a bowl of porridge, a
pile of clothes. Then add the question: 'What if?'
What if the apple rolled off the table on to the cat's
head and the cat leaped into the air, meowing, and
knocked over the bowl of porridge on to the pile of
freshly-ironed clothes and your mum went
ballistic?

*Ay caramba! Must tell Joan and Joan that Aunt Laura
sees them as mere objects. But honestly, what is she going
on about here? Apples? Porridge? Nothing more exciting
than a bit of spoiled ironing?*

I went to bed at last, flinging my exhausted self on to the fat
sleeping form of lazy, lounging old Xerxes, who had hidden
himself under Postman Pat's black and blue cat. He leaped
up screeching, hair standing on end. No namby-pamby
'meowing' for this mog. Why didn't he say he was going to
sleep there? I have a feeling this is going to be a tough week.

Nothing to report about the next six hours, due to sleeping. It's a shame you can't have some kind of dream-recorder
plugged into your brain, so a lot of interesting stuff about
what happened in the night is all ready and waiting for you
and not wasted.What a useful tool for an author that would
be. Must work on it.

After I got up, I came down to breakfast to find Howard and Candice deep in secret conversation, which stopped as soon as I entered in the kitchen. I let out a very loud sigh to express my disgust. I know I should confront them about their wicked plot to wreck Callum's life, but I just don't know how to talk about it.

There was a big envelope propped against a teapot shaped like a wheelie bin. I don't think this design will catch on. The envelope had a just-about-legible *Cordelia and Callum* written on it in Candice's awful handwriting.

Candice was smiling and nodding her head encouragingly. 'Little first-term-at-new-school treat for you both,' she said.

It's all very well to get lovey-dovey now the damage has been done, I thought. But I opened the envelope anyway.

GADZOOKS – IT'S RINGSIDE TICKETS FOR THE CIRCUS!

I love the circus. So does Callum. And we had heard that this big, exciting foreign one was coming to town but what with new schools and all this weird parental stuff, we had both forgotten about it. But Candice had remembered. Maybe she's not so bad after all.

'It's on Saturday afternoon,' Candice said, ruffling my hair. 'It's OK with Peter and Andrea; you and Callum can go together.'

'Aren't you coming?' I asked. It would be the first time we haven't all gone to the circus together.

Candice and Howard looked at each other. Was that a little secret smile I saw between them?

'No,' Candice said. 'We thought it would be nice for you and Callum, now you're at big school and so independent. And . . . we have some work stuff we absolutely have to do that afternoon. It would be much nicer for you to have something to do out of the house. But we thought we could make a day of it; we'll pick you up afterwards at seven, then take you both out somewhere nice for dinner.'

In the deepest dungeon of my suspicious mind, I began to smell a fatte ratte. Was this nice circus thing all it seemed to be? Or was it a way to get us out of the house all afternoon so Callum's dad could have his sordid affair?

'Anyway, I must be off, we're opening the gallery early today for a special customer. Fingers crossed, this might be the sale of the century. Bye.' Candice kissed Howard and me on top of our balding and spiky heads respectively and was gone in a blur, unaware of stepping on Xerxes's saucer of milk by the kitchen door and spilling it over his front paws. He growled and shook one milky paw at a time, wearing a very gloomy expression and undoubtedly wondering if it was too late to move house at his time of life.

Howard looked up from his book and gave me a daft smile while nodding his head in that 'should we talk about anything or leave each other in peace?' kind of way.

I decided to take ye ratte by the whiskers.

'How are Peter and Andrea? Haven't seen them for a while,' I commented casually, pushing cereal around my bowl.

Howard looked up from his book of ancient runes and

gazed at me blankly from behind his little half-moon specs.

'Er, fine, I think. I haven't seen them recently either.' And he turned back to his runes.

Aha! A clue. 'Why not?' I asked. (Oh so casual, an absolute preponderance of casualty.)

'Why?' he replied.

'Don't you usually have a drink with Peter most weeks?'

'Hmmm. He's busy, I suppose.'

I could have asked, 'Why is he seeing a girl young enough to be his daughter instead of Andrea and why are you encouraging him?' No. I couldn't do that. Cats would be among the pigeons, though, in Xerxes's case, this would admittedly have no ill effect at all.

'Why don't we have them round for a meal?' I suggested.

Howard sighed, put down his book and gazed at me with the tender fatherly gaze he uses about once a year if he thinks anything is wrong.

'What's up?' he asked. 'Are you missing Callum, now you're at Falmer North?'

'No, no. I still see him all the time.'

'Missing childhood? Want us all to meet up every week like we used to?'

'No . . .' (Yes, actually. I want to go back to a time when parents behaved like adults and did sensible things like tuck you up in bed and tell you lies about the tooth fairy. Hmmm. Must rethink this position.)

'It's a good idea. I'll ask them round next week. We need to catch up,' he said, going back to his book.

Well, that will be weird. What on earth would we all say to each other? But if Howard keeps his word, maybe that will be the time me and Callum could summon up the courage to expose them all. But would that be a good thing? Would it end in divorce? Surely I should confront Buff Babs herself and make her see how cruel she is being?

I forgot all this at school fortunately, mainly because Scarlet Woman Buff Barbara was nowhere to be found. She was probably off buying unspeakable items for her love tryst with Callum's dad. Also, my swanky new tights laddered all the way up both legs and the banshees asked why my designer relatives can't get me freebies. I wish I'd never done that stupid stuff with the burned shirt. I can't bear tights. I was better off as a tomboy with scabby knees. Soon it'll be tampons and lip-gloss too. All boys ever need is a razor and that's not for years.

Viola overheard the banshees talking about my designer relatives. 'Your life's so exciting,' she whispered delightedly to me. 'Famous writer for an aunt, famous fashion people in New York sending you the latest designs . . .'

'Look, that designer part's not true,' I told her. 'I feel stupid about it, because they all know it was a lie and they've been winding me up ever since. But I was just trying to make a good impression on the first day.'

'I understand,' Viola said. 'I felt the same on Day One. I just couldn't think of any way of doing it. It's easier to read a book and keep to yourself. But it's right about your Aunt Laura?'

She was looking at me anxiously. Aunt Laura is so much

a part of my life I didn't get what she meant at first. 'Oh yes, that's all true,' I said when the penny dropped. 'You'll meet her one day, I promise.'

Viola looked so relieved it was like I'd saved her from execution. 'Surely you didn't think I'd forged all those e-mails did you?'

'Well, I've seen people do much worse,' said Viola. I must have looked startled because she immediately added, 'You know, in films . . .'

'No. What do you mean?' I asked. 'Has something bad happened?'

'Everybody's got something bad in their lives . . . Look at your mate Callum's folks.'

'Yes. But what about YOU?'

She changed the subject quickly. 'Me? I'm going to the circus on Saturday,' she said. 'Would you like to come?'

'Sorry, I'm already going with Callum. Are you going with your folks?"

I threw this in casually, because I could see Viola's face fall when I mentioned Callum and I didn't like to think of her going on her own but I didn't want to share the circus with anyone but Callum.

'My mum, yes. My dad's . . . away.'

'Does he have to travel for work?'

'No. Yes. Not really.'

'It's just, you never mention him.' I summoned up my courage. 'Has he left? It's not unusual. In fact it's pretty standard round here. Most kids—'

'No. I don't want to talk about it.' Viola's cloud swelled above her.

'OK. Sorry. Maybe we can meet before it starts and say hello. It'll be nice to meet your mum. At the circus.' We stared at each other awkwardly. Viola's cloud was low and heavy.

Viola had said she only lived round the corner, but there's the toughest estate in the area there and as she hasn't asked me round yet I wonder if she lives on it. I couldn't help thinking that, if I pushed it, would she tell me stuff I don't really want to hear. I wondered if her dad was dead maybe. I always rabbit on about myself, but I'm not sure I want to know about Viola's problems – I'm busy enough with Callum's. I suppose I want her to be my friend I can talk about writing with, rather than problems, but I wonder if she knows that I do care about her. Viola broke the silence.

'Have you done any more of your story? It has to be in on Monday. I've done one about a Russian boy wizard who goes to a wizards' school and falls in love with a dying orphan girl. But he's rubbish at magic and so he can't save her life. It's called *Ivan the Terrible*.'

'Really?' I said. 'Is it ironic?'

'What's ironic?' Viola asked.

'Oh, er, sort of tongue-in-cheek. Like when you thought *The Lady of the Rings* was a parody. It doesn't matter. It's going to be great on Saturday at the circus, isn't it?' I said brightly.

Back home, I try to seek inspiration for The Greatest Novel Ever Written.

Look, I don't want to be mean to you, Dear Reader. I put that bit under Aunt Laura's tip in so you would think it was the pangram. But it isn't. I went back to rewriting my olde rubbishe when Callum called. I think I'm talking more to him now we've started secondary school than I did before. Shows you what A Crisis can do.

'You're not being overheard?' he asked me, in such a low voice I could hardly hear him at all, let alone get rumbled by anybody else.

'No. Howard and Candice are in a huddle in the living room. They're doing a lot of that nowadays,' I said. 'But Xerxes looks like he is listening. Just don't talk cat and we'll be OK.'

'MIAAAWWGHH!' Callum squawked loudly without warning down the phone, deafening me. Xerxes sloped off.

'Did he go?' Callum asked, returning to whispering.

'Yes, what did you say to him?'

'Sorry, can't tell you that until you're sixteen.'

'Ye vile clay-brained spoilsporte. What's happening?'

'Something's up. You know we're going to the circus together on Saturday?'

'Yes, isn't it great?'

'You think so? It's all part of a dastardly plot to get us out the way. Listen, I hid my minidisc recorder in Dad's study this evening, to catch him out on his secret phone calls. He called somebody up, but unfortunately I missed most of it because he decided to blimmin' well sit on the cushion the machine was hidden under.'

'A plague on't,' I whispered in awe.

'Right. But he got up just before the end. He was talking to someone on the phone. He was saying he had to keep his voice down in case they were discovered. And he gave an address to go to on Saturday afternoon.'

'Where?' I just about managed to ask.

'You'll never guess. Your place. They're going to meet at your place.'

I felt a cold shiver run down my spine. I couldn't say a word.

'Cordelia? Are you there? Did you know anything about this?'

It all came out. I couldn't bear him thinking I might some-how have been in on it too. I told him about the conversation Viola and I had overheard between Howard and Candice. I said I had wanted to tell him but felt I had to hear their side of the story first. I apologised to him every way I could for having such Traitorous Poltroons for parents. He was very understanding.

'I know. Somebody ought to give us a choice in the parents we get. But it's not too late. If Saturday's when it's all happening, then it's up to me to do something about it.'

'Me too. It's my parents' fault as much as it is your dad's. We have to show them the error of their ways, shame them back on to the true path, offer them the hope and optimism of youth and all that.'

'We can meet at the circus, and catch the first half. We'll have to skip out early if my plan's going to work, though,' Callum said gloomily. 'And it's all their fault.'

'There'll be other circuses,' I told him. 'But you've only got one set of parents.'

I think I might have heard a little sniff from Callum before he hung up.

I went back to my room to drown, lose and forget myself in my book, instead of thinking of all this horrible real life drama.

The story so far: Lothario, faithful servant of Lady Cordelia, has undressed her while she was asleep and dressed up in her clothes. (Note to self: described like this, The Greatest Novel Ever Written doesn't quite sound like the fairy-tale romance I had intended. I'm afraid it's been infected by the loutish behaviour of my elders and betters. Must clean it up and ensure readers do not jump to dodgy conclusions.)

Pretending to be Lady C, Lothario has dispatched Prince Kevin, the first of the princes come to claim her hand in marriage and stop her fulfilling her dream to be an artist.

When I win the story competition and my book is selling faster than hot cakes (though I've never met anybody who waits in a demented queue outside bakers' shops waiting for the hot cakes to go on sale – I suppose this is a cliché) you will truly see, Dear Reader, how moving Lothario's devotion is to his beautiful trapped mistress of youthful passions and tumbling golden tresses, and how anybody who thinks there's anything rude about this dressing and undressing part deserves to have their foulle braine washed out with soap.

What happens next is that Lothario has to put Lady C's clothes back on her, and I've had lots of scary, suspenseful and clever things happening to make this very exciting – like her falling out of bed but him flinging himself underneath her body as a devoted mattress just in time, and then singing sweet lullabies to her to make her think she's back in her idyllic nursery of olde, making creaking and splashing and whistling-wind noises while he's rolling her from side to side to make her think she's dreaming she's on a boat to a Magicke Island, and even (a Great Leape of Literary Genius this, although I say it myself) being the ghostly voice of Michael Angelo telling her she is the greatest artiste in the world after him. I've heard Michael Angelo was very good at painting ceilings (ask your teacher if you haven't heard of him, I know all this stuff because of Callum's great artistic talent). Anyway, Lady C smiles a smile of pure happiness and sighs a long sigh which makes Lothario's hearte melte.

Then she wakes up just after he's done up the last pearly button, and ye booke goes on:

The Lady of the Rings (ctd)

'Lothario, thank Heaven you are by my side.'

'Thank you, Heaven,' says Lothario obediently.

'Lothario, I must flee this place. For there will be another prince, and another, and another after that and one doome laden daye they will wear me down and then what will become of my art?' cried the Lady Cordelia, suddenly realising the awful truth of her situation once more, as it thrust itself upon her.

'But you have ruined your luscious garments,' cried Lothario.

'No, my paints have done it! It is a sign! My art is beckoning to me, telling me that all the frills and finery and flammery and frippery in the world mean as nought by comparison!'

Nurse Ruby tottered in and sank into a deep profound curtsey, her anciente wrinkled knees crumbling and squeaking like olde hinges as she did so.

'My darling little The Lady Cordelia, that I have coddled since you were but a mere whiffet, a tiny bantling, that I have fed with puréed fruits and mashed meats and spices from all the four corners of our great kitchen—'

'Yes, yes, get on with it, my art is calling me and I must fly,' said The Lady Cordelia impatiently.

'I beg you, I implore you, I ask you with all the strength at my disposal, to reconsider your decision, for there are three more fine princes at the door. And after that there will be three more and yet three more and yet three more. You must not be like your aunt, my Lady, who turned down the noble and filthy rich Prince Lupin for that crazed varlet – ye foolishe, fawninge, flap-mouthed flap-dragon Frederick Fol-de-rol. Ye noble Lupin owned all of Scotland and half of France, he bought her diamonds, dreames and undying devotion yet your strumpet aunt spurned him. Crazy Frederick bought many very exquisite opal jewels. Your harpy aunt was a sucker for opals and ended her dayes as a washerwoman in the Hebrides, with naught but an goat for company.'

The Lady Cordelia waited until Nurse Ruby drew a wheezy breathe before she declared, 'I will go alone into ye worlde and make my owne living by selling paintings made of earthe and oiles and flamingoe feathers and I will use ye boughs of oaken trees for brushes and the very oaken leaves themselves will be my gown.'

'But harken a moment, my Lady,' Nurse Ruby creaked once more into speech, her anciente tongue, lips and tonsils quivering with the effort. 'And I will tell you of the splendiferous charms of the three heroic young millionaires who are e'en now galloping passionately hither on steeds of fire.'

(Beginning to think this stuff is a bit too good for crumbling old Nurse Thingy. Aunt Laura would definitely tell me it's important to keep people in character. Think I'll write Nursey down a bit in the final draft. Alas and Alack, how hard is the life of a writer. In words, alas, drown I.)

Chapter Six

Ye Real Life Is Not Like Ye Movies

Laura Hunt's Top Tips for Budding Writers:
Cast your characters as if your book is a film. Pick an actor for each of your characters, and imagine them saying your words. This will help you visualise them as real people.

Lothario: Johnny Depp? Too old. Orlando Bloom?
Joaquin Phoenix. Yes!
Lady C: Angelina Jolie? Keira Knightley?
Nurse Ruby: Dame Judi Dench! Yay, verily.

Woke up on Saturday having had a horrible dream about my parents kissing. This appeared in a fat thought-bubble inside my head and wouldn't go away. They were making slurping sounds, like hippos in mud. I had never thought about it before and it left a strange taste in my mouth – a mix of liquorice and Pritt Stick. Do all those old people you see on buses kiss each other when nobody's watching? How weirdly weird. But still, it is a lot better than thinking of Callum's dad kissing Buff Barbara.

Not sure what Callum has in mind for later, but he said he'd taken a lot of his savings out from the wallet hidden amongst his boxer shorts, so it must be something big. It's a proper romantic mission, to Save Souls from Perdition, wherever that is.

Not knowing what else to do to help, I went to the stationer's after school yesterday (my favourite shop, not that I'd dare own up to it to anyone but you, Dear Reader) for some fantastic flimsy sugar-pink paper, a bit like Aunt Laura's book jackets in fact, and some lilac-scented ink. Smells a bit like loo cleaner, but it looks nice. I'd thought of forging a letter from the foul Buff Barbara – she who was going to betray Andrea under my very own roof – something like this:

> *Dearest adored beloved one,*
> *All is discovered. We must flee, the two of us, to the four*
> *corners of the earth. Better to lose our love forever and never*
> *again feel our hearts beating frantically like the wings of wild*
> *birds entwined for eternity, than be caged, my love, in this*
> *hell-hole of suburbia. A thousand kisses on your glorious*
> *manly brow.*

I read it out to Callum over the phone, and he pointed out a vital flaw in it my romantic writerly self had not noticed.

'Well, it means he'll just go away to the four corners of the earth, doesn't it?'

'Yes, but they won't be together doing all that betraying and treachery, will they?' I said.

'Ummm. Not sure I wouldn't rather have him around betraying and stuff than not here at all. Anyway, it's not very realistic.'

I spent minutes on the bloody love letter and what thanks do I get?

'Anyway,' Callum said. 'My plan is better. See you at the circus. We'll take it from there. Don't forget the keys to your house.'

Well, I wouldn't. But why does it matter to him?

The other thing I spent a lot of last night doing was bringing The Greatest Novel Ever Written towards its exciting climax.

The Lady of the Rings is what real love is all about, none of this schmoozing around in bars and the houses of your alleged best friends. What a wonderful romance The Greatest Novel Ever Written is. No one else in the class will get anywhere near it in Mrs Parsing's writing competition.

The rest of Saturday seemed to crawl by, but finally it was time to go and meet Callum at the entrance to the park where the circus was. Howard and Candice dropped me off at quarter past four.

'We'll pick you up here at seven – we'll be busy till then,' Candice said, rather shiftily. Hmmm, we'll see about that, I thought.

We soon saw Viola with her mum, who looks even more shy and retiring than Viola does. I introduced Viola and Callum. They went through a big 'heard a lot about you' thing, and I noticed myself having a very brief funny feeling inside at the thought that they might fancy each other. Viola ended up sitting quite near us, and I occasionally caught Callum's head turned in her direction.

'We'll see the first bit,' Callum hissed to me. 'Then we'll activate Plan A.'

The circus started with everybody running into the ring waving their arms about, turning cartwheels, springing up and down ropes, swirling cloaks and shouting mysterious foreign things, then the clowns came on bumping into each other, firing guns that blew out confetti and flags, making water squirt out of each other's ears and so on. Then two people who looked as if they were wearing sprayed-on silver costumes started dancing a very slow ballet dance on ropes about a million feet up in the roof of the tent.

'That's really beautiful,' I said, as much to myself as Callum.

'It's time to go,' is all Callum said in reply as he pulled my arm.

With people grumbling and fussing as we climbed over them to get out, and the crowd gasping when the dancing couple in the roof tottered when we clutched one of their supporting ropes on the way over the barrier, Callum and I made for the exit. Viola saw us and looked startled. Callum caught her eye and gave her a 'what can you do?' shrug and a smile – a bit of a cool move for people who've only just met, I would have said.

'Got any feathers?' Callum asked me as we ran up the road in the direction of the high street.

'No, I just came out like this,' I said. 'Is Plan A that we disguise ourselves as chickens and peck them into submission?'

'Nah, it's for a booby trap.'

As we hit Bloggs's DIY Emporium, I began to get the point. Callum produced his savings and we gathered together:

Three plastic buckets;

One big pot of instant glue;

Lots of rope;

Four fire alarms;

Two garden hoses with sprinklers;

One desk fan and

One large box of matches.

Having bought all that, and with the Bloggs manager having given us the same suspicious look he gives everybody, even if they've only gone in for a light bulb, we ran as fast as we could with the extra baggage to my house. Callum revealed he also had some horrible battery-powered screaming skulls left over from Halloween, and some joke shop smoke bombs that are only supposed to be sold to the over-sixteens. I don't know how he does it.

'Better go in the back way,' I said to Callum, 'in case Howard and Candice didn't go out after all.'

We went down the alleyway behind the houses, over the fence and crept up the back garden. There was no sign of life in the house. On tiptoe, we let ourselves in the back door. I trod on lazy Xerxes of course, who was asleep in his basket in the kitchen, with one leg unwisely hanging out. This time he didn't even hiss, but growled, rather sadly.

The house was definitely empty. But. Oh. The. Horror. The horror.

Candice and Howard had tidied up. In fact it looked like a firm of cleaners might have been in. And there were red roses and a heart-shaped balloon in the hall.

'They've made it nice for them,' said Callum, his voice cracking. I wanted to give him a hug. I felt so ashamed that my parents could be encouraging the break-up of Callum's family.

'It won't look so nice in an hour's time,' I said grimly.

We set to work.

We started by running the garden hoses through the windows of the kitchen and living room and plugged them into the outside taps. The cackling Halloween skulls were put at the top of the stairs. We perched one of the buckets among the ornaments above the front door, full of cold water and hooked to the opening door by Callum's complicated SAS-style rope arrangement. He laid the smoke bombs up the stairs, with the fire alarms scattered high on bookcases and cupboards on the landings.

'Now for your mum and dad's bedroom,' he cackled. 'If they're keen enough to get past this lot, that'll be the killer punch.'

I dreaded finding a sign saying, H*ello, young lovers* on the door of the – aaargh! – master bedroom . . . But it looked pretty normal, if scarily tidy.

We hung a laundry bag from the ceiling light, which we filled with feathers mercilessly ripped from inside Candice's nice flouncy pillows. Tough. We put the desk fan on a chair, just under the bag of feathers, and plugged it into the wall in place of the nice romantic floor lights that you turn on as you come in. Then we filled the other bucket with water, tied one end of the rope to it, stretched the other end over the open wardrobe door and tied it to the bottom of the feather bag. We didn't watch *Home Alone* for nothing. The finishing touch was to get into the corridor and balance the bucket and the pot of glue on top of the partly-open bedroom door, a tricky business performed on tiptoe on a chair – several times we almost fell off and booby-trapped ourselves instead.

But suddenly we heard voices. Callum and I ran into my bedroom, and when I looked out of the window my heart nearly jumped out through my mouth. 'Oh no. Look!'

It was only six-thirty but the real action was already starting. My worst fears were confirmed. I'd been secretly hoping it had all been a mistake, that the girl in the pub had just been a Buff Barbara look-alike. But no. Callum's dad was coming up the front path, and so was a loudly-giggling Buff Barbara. Definitely her. They were both carrying what looked like a million bulging shopping bags.

Callum didn't say a word, only stared at them.

'Get down!' I squawked. 'They'll see you!'

Moving as slowly as if he was about five hundred years old, Callum finally dropped to his knees. 'What are all those bags for?' he said ponderously. 'Are they moving in? Is this it? My dad and a sixteen-year-old are going to start a new life in your house?' He looked at me as if it was my fault.

'Come on!' I hissed, dragging Callum by the arm. 'If they are, it's time we put them off!'

As we ran out on to the upstairs landing, we heard the key turning in the lock. Crouching behind the banisters, we watched with bated breath as the door opened and Peter came in, struggling with the bags. Gadzooks, the bucket hadn't moved an inch! May a blizzard of poisoned red-hot needles fall upon the treacherous scriptwriters of *Home Alone*! In came Buff Barbara with all their worldly goods, undoubtedly bagfuls of satin sheets and see-through boxers and lap dancer knickers and dodgy DVDs, and the bucket just stayed hanging up there without a care in the world. Would all our plans come to naught?

'What shall we do?' Callum asked me, looking defeated for the first time that day.

'Regroup,' I told him. We went back into my bedroom, locked the door and sat on the bed quaking. We could just hear the Horrible Pair banging about in the kitchen below, laughing. Oh my God, I thought, suppose they start Doing It before we can stop them! Would a traumatised (Peter would love that word) Callum suddenly turn into a Complete Loony and have to be carted off foaming at the mouth? Would all my romantic dreams be smashed and I'd wake up tomorrow morning a crack addict in a bin liner?

Ages seemed to pass. It was like we were turned to stone, unable to decide what to do. We heard a lot more noises downstairs but shut them out.

'When they get to the bedroom they'll really get the treatment,' I said, to comfort Callum. 'There's no way all that stuff won't work.'

'Suppose they don't even go to the bedroom?' Callum wailed.

'All right, then!' I shouted, not bothered now if we were found out. 'Let's set the rest off and get out of here!'

Moving like greased lightning (Panic-stricken note to self: must find out one day what on earth that actually means) we raced out on to the landing. The downstairs hall was empty, the bags were gone. A lot of laughter was still coming from the kitchen, and it was even more horrible than before, with Peter's laugh seeming to sound deeper and darker and drunk one minute and hysterical and squeaky the next, and Buff Barbara's laugh sounding older and ruder. The bucket still hung boringly over the door.

We hurtled downstairs, lighting the smoke bombs as we went. Callum flicked the switches on the Halloween skulls and they started flashing horrible red bloody teeth and squealing. I stepped on the cowering Xerxes, who was at the foot of the stairs, hair on end as usual. The fire alarms started letting off wild screams as the smoke from the smoke bombs rose, turning my brain to scrambled eggs – the noise they made, in combination with the Halloween masks, made us put our hands over our ears and start screaming too.

Even though the hall was filling with smoke, we would be seen by the Horrible Couple any moment, once they disentangled to investigate the din, and the front door was the only way out. We wrenched it open and fled into the garden, hearing a shout of 'Fire!' behind us, and vaguely realising that the bucket of water had finally responded and poured all over the pursuing, terrified – now drenched – and far from lazy Xerxes. Hell's bells! Mysterious grown-ups turned in at the front gate! We veered sharply left and ran between the houses towards the back garden, falling over the hoses draped out of the kitchen window as we went.

'Might as well finish the job,' Callum grimaced, picking himself up. We turned on the taps, to the gratifying sound of screaming and cursing inside.

And then we stopped, panting, and stared at each other.

It was an awful lot of screaming and cursing for two people. And it sounded like an awful lot of different voices doing it.

Very slowly, we stood on tiptoe and raised our heads above the windowsill. It was difficult to see much in the kitchen for the spray of the sprinklers, but a lot of people seemed to be in there, flapping about and trying to find the way out.

'Gadzooks,' we said, at the same time, as the kitchen emptied.

'Cease fire,' I whispered to Callum. I didn't know what

had gone wrong, but something was certainly weird about this. We turned the water off and dragged the hoses out through the window. In all the confusion, no one saw this. In the distance, the fire alarms were still wailing.

A long time seemed to pass. Nobody came.

'Maybe we should go back to my place,' Callum said. 'And have a think.'

It was a good idea, but like most things that afternoon, it didn't work. We went back to the front path and ran into three things:

1) A very wet and angry Xerxes, who'd obviously been waiting for my return to deliver a whole stream of violent, spitting, hair-on-end complaints about his treatment.
2) Several big firemen, carrying a hose.
3) Howard, Candice and . . . Andrea.

'My God!' Candice said, wringing her hands. 'What the hell's going on?' 'Then she saw us. 'Thank God! Where have you two been? We waited outside the circus for half an hour! I've been sick with worry.'

The firemen went in with the hose. Almost all the smoke had gone by now, the fire alarms had stopped and only the Halloween masks, though their batteries were almost dead, were making a small whimpering sound. People were milling about in the hall, looking puzzled. Peter came out, scratching his head.

A fireman came out too, carrying one of Callum's smoke bombs and a dying Halloween mask.

'You got any kids?" he asked, rather sarcastically, to Howard and Peter.

'Err . . . yes,' they both replied, despondently.

'Maybe you should have a word with them,' the fireman said, and then all the firemen trooped off back to the three, yes, three, fire engines, muttering.

Howard, Candice, Peter and Andrea stared at Callum and me. Peter and Andrea stared at each other. We stared back at all of them, speechless.

Eventually, Howard spoke, very quietly. 'Any particular reason you'd like to share with us about why you decided to ruin the party?'

'Party?' Callum and I stuttered.

'Party?' Andrea stuttered too.

'Party,' Howard said. 'It's Peter's surprise anniversary party for Andrea. Only it isn't a surprise now. It's a catastrophe.'

'Well . . .' I started.

'Well, what?'

'Well . . . I heard you telling Candice that Peter wanted to celebrate his love,' I said, quietly. 'You were going to let them meet here rather than a hotel.'

'And you kept making secret phone calls,' Callum added, looking at his dad.

'And we saw you kissing Barbara in a pub,' I said to Peter, still shocked at the thought.

There was a long silence.

'I wanted it to be a surprise,' Peter said to Andrea, who – forsooth! Five-, six-, seven-sooth! – was beginning to smile.

The George Clooney figure and about fifty other wet and sniffling people – some of whom were still coughing – staggered out of out house and gave Andrea a hug. The last of these was Buff Barbara, who gave Andrea an absolutely huge hug.

'Barbie! Darling!' Andrea squealed. 'Did you organise this?'

'Well, it was mainly Mum and Dad,' Barbara said, indicating George Clooney and a much older version of Buff Barbara, who was also wearing a miniskirt but without quite the same effect. 'And you must be Callum,' said Buff Barbara. 'My you've grown.'

Callum stood frozen like a rabbit in headlights, except for a faint wiggling of his ears. 'So you're *Barbie*,' he muttered. And one by one the pieces of this jigsaw clunked slowly into place in my brain-dead brain. It turned out Buff Babs was Andrea's oldest friend's daughter, who had just returned from ten years in Spain. So Callum hadn't seen her or her parents (Clooney and neanderthal miniskirt) since she was six. He'd have been two, which explained why he hadn't recognised any of them, of course.

'But why didn't you TELL us?' Callum and I wailed, as one.

'I can see now, that that was a mistake,' said Peter. 'But I couldn't keep a secret at your age and I was desperate to keep it a surprise.'

'We weren't going to leave you out,' explained Howard.

'That's why we came to pick you up at the circus. We were going to arrive here with Andrea and you two and surprise you all at once.'

'We should have told them, then they wouldn't have ruined everything,' said Candice.

Callum and I often used to cry at the same time when we were little, and I think that was, at that moment, about to happen again. Except that George Clooney put an arm around each of us.

'I think there's been an understandable mistake,' he said. 'And the best way of putting it behind us is to go and have a party.'

Well, it all goes to show what a little bit too much imagination can do. It can turn an innocent conversation about how to help a friend into a dastardly plot, or a friendly embrace into a fully-fledged kiss, for instance, but I'll tell you all about the party and other disasters in the next chapter because first I've got to fill you in quickly on my Great Novel.

The story so far: Ageing Nurse Ruby is just about to tell The Lady C about the splendiferous charms of the three heroic young millionaires who are e'en now galloping passionately hither on steeds of fire (which I'm going to tone down a bit so Nurse Ruby doesn't get more interesting than the central characters).

It goes on with Nurse Ruby talking to The Lady C.

The Lady of the Rings (ctd)

'The oldest, Prince Zircon, son of Queen Doris of Dorset, is offering you sixteen golden palaces, one for each month of the year with four spare, a hundred golden horses and a string of elephants each bearing caskets laden with jewels and gowns in spun gold.'

'I care not for gold,' said The Lady Cordelia, turning her back on the nurse.

'The middle brother, Prince Hyacinth, is offering you twenty-six silver palaces - one for every fortnight, and a stable of silver horses bearing exquisite gowns of the finest silver thread spun by the silver silk worms of Saffron Walden.'

'I care not for silver,' said The Lady Cordelia defiantly, stamping her maidenly foote.

'That is why you will like Prince Conrad,' wheedled the nurse, her old bones creaking with the effort of talking for so long. 'He comes riding to our castle on naught but an humble donkeye. He brings gifts of plaited rushes, woven into your name, love poetry painted by his own hand on tiny pebbles that he has himself collected from the babbling brooks and distant ocean shores, and a set of paint brushes that he has made especially for you from the hairs of red squirrels that he has lovingly nourished by hand and played to on his flute until they, by their own free will, have given him a pawful of their precious haires each. Moreover, he has himself ground from the earth and rocks and pebbles and clay the finest natural dyes and mixed them with the most perfect natural oils to produce the finest set of oil paints the world has ever seen.'

'He sounds not bad, as it goes,' quoth the lovely Lady C, springing up, 'but I cannot marry Prince Conrad, Prince Hyacinth, Prince Zircon, Prince Kevin or any other prince. For I love another!'

'You love another?' asked old faithful Nurse Ruby, and youthful, manly, handsome Lothario, as one.

'You mean you love your art, Ladysheep, naturally,' said Lothario, his voice trembling in a tremulous way.

'NO! NO! It is YOU (no, better to use 'thee' here, for anciente romantic impact) that I love, my own Lothario. And I know thou lovest me too. We will fly tonight' (Dear Reader, this does not mean they will hop on an Easyjet to Ibiza; it is a medieval way of saying they'll go somewhere in a big hurry) 'and start a new life together on an island paradise somewhere over the rainbow, way up high.' (Note to self: think of somewhere else for that, or may get sued by big movie company.)

Chapter Seven

Whoops

The party for Andrea and Peter was wonderful, except for a little hiccup I'll tell you about in a minute . . .

The longer it all went on, and the more glasses of champagne Andrea and Peter's well-wishers had, the funnier they seemed to find the Noble Crusade of me and Callum. Even the ones who got wet, or thought they were having a heart attack when the Halloween masks and fire alarms went off, ended up thinking it was all hilarious. And fortunately the water in the kitchen had missed most of the food.

'Thought old Pete was having an affair,' they chortled. 'Bloody marvellous. Chance'd be a fine thing.'

Peter made a soppy speech about love that made everyone cry (although it might have been the lingering effects of the smoke bombs) and everybody sang to Peter and Andrea at about midnight. It was very touching, even if they all seemed to be singing different things.

Buff Barbara turned out to be seriously cool. She said it had been tough coming back to England and starting Year Eleven and that Falmer North had been a bit of a shock after her strict Spanish school, but that the kids were OK and most of the teachers, too. She said I should do Spanish, then she could coach me. So now I have a friend in Year Eleven. Hah!

The party went on into the small hours so Callum stayed over, on a sleeping bag on my floor. Glad to say I also made peace with Xerxes, who came to sleep on top of Callum and almost managed to summon up a purr.

'Thou churlish clapper-clawed clotpole,' I said.

'Thou beslubbering beetle-headed baggage,' he replied (not Xerxes, Callum). But in a nice way. And we fell asleep as one.

There was, however, one small setback at about three o'clock in the morning.

We woke to the sound of screams, curses, crashes, and bangs from my parents' bedroom. Callum and I leaped up in terror to their door.

Horrible memories started coming back just before we took in the sight before us. Memories of propping a bucket of water and a pot of glue over the bedroom door. Memories of tying a bag of feathers from the ceiling, next to an electric fan.

Drenched, and covered in feathers, Howard and Candice would have looked like a couple of Disneyland actors pretending to be Donald Duck after a paddle – except that Howard had a plastic bucket on his head, and Candice was only wearing one high-heeled shoe, some rather fancy underwear I didn't even know she owned, and a massive, terrifying red blotch down one side of her face, which made my heart skip a beat. Howard snatched the bucket off, said a couple of exciting words you will all recognise but which unfortunately cannot be included in this book for Parental Anxiety reasons, then caught sight of his tottering, sticky, half-dressed, feather-clad wife. It thankfully became clear that the horrible mark on her face was actually one of Howard's natty red socks. It must have been in the bottom of the laundry bag, and the fan and the glue had done the rest.

Fortunately it was Howard who started laughing first. Then I did, then Callum did. Candice was on the verge of exploding with fury, but caught sight of herself in the dressing-table mirror. Howard quacked at her – a pretty good duck impression for a medieval scholar. She fell on to the bed, squealing, quacking and sometimes clucking hysterically.

'Go away, Cordelia,' Howard said between quacks. 'Your mother is having an identity crisis which needs my urgent attention.'

We went out and closed the door. The clucking went on for ages. I don't think I understand grown-ups. With anyone but Callum this would have been hideously embarrassing, but being more tired than I can ever remember being in my life, I found I didn't care.

In fact I didn't care about anything at all except suddenly realising that it was midday on Sunday. Gadzooks! My story has to be entered in the writing competition tomorrow!

Callum had left a note on my pillow. Sellotaped to the note was a rusty nail.

THANK THEE, VERILY. *If you ever want to stop being my frend, plees dont tel me as it wood be to paneful. Just stik this nale throo yor nose and I will get the messidge.*

I gulped.

I crawled downstairs to find the whole place gleaming. No water in sight, but there was a note from Candice propped against a strange new cauliflower-shaped teapot.

You owe Callum one. He tidied up at dawn. Me and Howard have gone to sauna to recover. xx

Still, lackaday. I am going to have to finish The Greatest Novel Ever Written somehow and get it written out in best. It'll take all day.

Wait, I've got to find some tips about how to write endings!

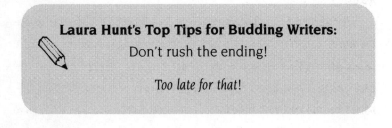

Laura Hunt's Top Tips for Budding Writers:
Don't rush the ending!

Too late for that!

So, here's how I finished it. I hope you agree it is très, très romantique. Lady Cordelia has just shocked anciente Nurse Ruby by declaring her undying devotion to Lothario, butt dancer.

The Lady of the Rings (ctd)

'NO! NO! It is THEE that I love, my own Lothario. And I know thou lovest me too!'

Lothario threw himself into another frenzy of excitement. 'Your Ladysheep! No! I am a married man! I am married to Isabella. I 'ave six cheeldren. And another on ze way.'

'Nonsense. You would have told me sooner.'

But alas and woe, 'twas the very troth.

'It is true, my pet, my angel, my cherub,' said Nurse Ruby, weeping. 'Isabella the twelfth housemaid to the under-gardener was betrothed to Lothario at the tender age of thirteen and they have been married these seven years by my reckoning. They have six bonnie babes: Pippin, Poppet, Percy, Pansy ...' (Note to reader: you could get married at my age back in anciente times, but of course you would be ded soon after so people made hay while they could.)

'AAAAEEEEEEEEEIIIIIIIIIOOOOOOOOOOOOOOOOOOOO OOOUUUUUUUUUUUUUUUWWWWWWWWWWWWWWW,' screamed The Lady Cordelia in anguish. (She then does this a couple more times, even louder, though it's very hard to write this down in words. Must look at some horror books about foulle murders and chainsaws, etc, to see how people usually write it out. Maybe there's a way of writing it like music, with those scrawly marks they have to show things getting louder.)

Lothario and even Nurse Ruby, who was normally deaf as a post – cliché watch: why post? Deaf as doorknob? Table? Pair of gloves? Ham sandwich? – are forced to put their hands over their ears and so do not hear the clamour of the nine hundred and fifty-seven faithful retainers and three noble princes as they race up the spiral staircase and burst into the Lady Cordelia's boudoir. This is a very dramatic scene, with lots of people screaming and wailing and gasping for breath in the crush and all the princes begging for ye hande of Lady C.

Above the din comes the tragicke screame of ye Lady Cordelia, feeling the fragile ruins of the remnants of her happiness tumbling down around her shell-like ears.

'I will have none of you if I cannot have he whom I love,' she says, and so saying she sped across the jumbled retainers. Despite all their efforts to restrain her, she cast her eyes imploringly with one last tragic plea at the youthful Lothario and with one bound threw herself out of the diamond-shaped boudoir window and plunged headlong into the freezing waters of the chill, deep and mysterious moat below. The deep, freezing, mysterious waters and the grasping tendrils of the boggy weevil-wort closed over her fragile form, leaving only her small white hand visible, pointing up out like the hand of the lady in the lake. There was a thrashing and a rippling on the still dark waters as the hideous finned beasts, slavitars and behemoths and

lurking banghas that lurked deep within the moat, swum eagerly, licking their lips and fangs, towards their prey.

*   And so ends the story of The Lady of the Rings, who lived for her art and died for her love.*

THE END.

Dunnit! But the final sentence had put me in mind of Xerxes and Blue.

I popped down to feed them both. Blue looking quite chirpy. The fire alarms and smoke had obviously cheered up his lonely life. But of course he had no one to tell about it. I reminded myself to buy him a friend tomorrow.

Chapter Eight

Ye Ende is Nighe

I woke up with billions of possibilities of how to make my story better, only to realise it was too late. I spent all day yesterday typing it out on the computer. Mrs Parsing said handwritten was OK, but mine had so many comments and notes to myself that I had to remove. Had to hand it in TODAY. My head felt hot, like fudge soup, and my hair had turned into muesli. Or toffee. No, actually a Mars bar had melted into it. I tried using a Brillo pad to get it out and ended up cutting most of my fringe off, so now I look like the Artful Dodger. In fact, like two artful dodgers. Am seeing double. Did someone spike my Coke at the party, or is this double vision pneumonia?

I had just stuffed the book into a magnificent pink folder and the next thing I knew my head had exploded and my legs had gone as flimsy as string. I tottered into the kitchen to see Candice trying to drink from a tea cup shaped like the Eiffel Tower (you have to suck the tea out as if it were a straw. It's no wonder these things don't sell). She took one look at me and gave a maternal squeak. She only ever makes this sound when I am ill. She put her hand on my forehead and said 'Bed'.

'But it's the writing competition deadline today!' I heard a voice croak. It sounded like ye ominous toade of doome, but it was me.

'Get a friend to take it in,' said Candice.

Thank ye goddes for Saint Viola. She was over on winged sandals clutching her own precious folder, took one look at me, screamed, fled up to my bedroom, scooped up my folder ('It's the pink one, on my bed,' I had croaked feebly) and Viola, now clutching two precious folders, blew me a kiss and sped off.

Hope she doesn't get a late detention; Falmer North gets more like a prison every day. They have electronic gadgets whirring in the form tutors' underpants or something telling them how many times you are late and probably sending your photograph to MI5. Now she might get a letter sent home.

Still, my book looked excellent. Have written *The Lady of the Rings* on the front in seven shades of purple and *Cordelia Lucinda Arbuthnott* in pink, just a tad smaller, to look modest.

This was the last thing I remember thinking before falling back into bed and sleeping the deep sleep of those who have stayed up too long and got over-excited, not to mention soaked to the skin and caught in criminal acts.

Have now spent nearly a WEEK in bed, which hasn't happened since I was five. Spent it planning alternative endings to my Great Work. The competition result is announced on Monday and I am going to school then if it kills me.

When I turn *The Lady of the Rings* into a whole book I will have Lady C getting out of the lake (maybe rescued by mermaids?) and going on adventures. She will slay some hydras, trick minotaurs and all that and then make paintings of her exploits. She might marry eventually, but only when she has fulfilled her ambition as an artist and her heart has mended from Lothario's scorching blow.

Or should Lothario flee his wife and kids to be with her, realising he loves her after all? Then she could reject him, saying, 'Return to your little chickadees, my own, my darling. For though I will never love another but you, I cannot break the heart of a sister in struggle, your wife, who, though plain as a pike staff and with boils to boot, has borne you seven children and even now weeps of a broken heart.'

Maybe the plain boil-encrusted wife could die in childbirth and they could live happily ever after. Not the wife, of course. But could Lady C be happy as the stepmother of seven? I can't really kill off all the kiddies too . . . Aunt Laura would tell me off about this, because it should be Lady Cordelia who is plain and boil-encrusted and the wife should be beautiful but cruel, so that True Love overcomes mere things like boils, by looking deep into the soul beneath. But does that happen in real life? Gadzooks, this writing lark is tricky, you keep having to listen to your conscience instead of going for cheap thrills.

Maybe Lady C should choose the rich prince, just to spite Lothario, then realise that Prince Conrad is her true love? Or, could she meet another artist in the dark misty ominous mountains beyond the Enchanted Forest and sit for her portrait? He would turn out to be Leonardo da Vinci and they could live happily ever after. Lady Cordelia could be the Mona Lisa! Or I could reveal that SHE, the Lady Cordelia herself, painted the Mona Lisa as a self-portrait. Imagine the local paper:

> *Girl writer discovers real Mona Lisa in medieval feminist saga!*
> *This superlatively imaginative tale weaves together high romance and rip-roaring adventure as The Lady Cordelia Arbuthnott faces ogres, giants and monsters but, most devastatingly, the well of loneliness that is at the very heart of each of us in her quest to discover herself through her art. However, true love prevails in this stirring historical work of fiction.*

Have a feeling Leonardo da Vinci was gay, though.

Writing stories is tricky, there are so many possible endings.

Laura Hunt's Top Tips for Budding Writers:

The ending should feel as though it were inevitable, the one and only possible ending the book should have. Try to end on a note of HIGH reader satisfaction.

See? Exactly the opposite of what I've been thinking. Will the reader be satisfied with mine? I suppose if they hate Lady C they will be thrilled that she has hurtled to her doome.

Feel the need for a Mars bar – a sure sign of recovery.

Competition result today. Zoomed to school on winged trainers as worn by ye winged godde Mercury himself.

They made us wait all day. Viola and I could hardly speak for the tension and in the end I sneaked into the library five minutes before we were supposed to and there were the results, pinned on the noticeboard!

<u>*Romance*</u>:
First prize: *Viola Larpent for* Ivan the Terrible.
Second prize: *Mathadi Osunbor for* My Heart Goes On.
Third Prize: *Toby Fairweather for* Whatever.

I didn't even bother to look at the other categories. I just stood there with my mouth opening and closing very s-l-o-w-l-y, like Blue, when he's depressed. It wasn't possible, was it? Tobylerone had got third prize! In romance! There must be some mistake! Where were the runners up?

I became aware of a presence just behind me. The presence stooped and a voice very like a bear murmured in my ear. 'Was your story in a pink folder?'

It was Tobylerone, aka Toby Fairweather, prize-winning author of W*hatever*.

'Yes, why?'

'Well, I saw your mate nicking it off the pile of entries. Didn't want to grass or nothing, but it does run in her family.'

'What? Who do you mean?'

'Viler. Her old man's Fizzy Oake. He's a legend down our way,' said Toby.

'What do you mean?' I asked.

'He's inside.'

'Inside what?'

Tobylerone rolled his eyes. Ye troth dawned.

'You mean Viola's dad is in prison?'

'Shhhhh.'

Mrs Parsing swept in, followed by the rest of our English class. Viola came towards me, grinning. I turned away.

'Congratulations!' came the familiar boom of Mrs Parsing. 'Splendid entries! The three category winners will all be published in the Falmer Gazette. Gareth, your story was blood-curdling. Your descriptions of low-life and the criminal underclass were most dramatic and convincing. I admire your research. *Toxic Psycho* has won the thriller section hands down. Well done!' I turned to look for 'Gareth' and was amazed to see Snort grinning wolfishly and being patted on the back by dudes in hoodies. He looked about as much like my idea of a writer as Tobylerone did. But Parsing was now talking about the romance winner: 'Yours, Viola, was a masterpiece, or should I say mistresspiece, of tenderness. The final scene, where the polar ice cap is melting and Ivan, adrift on the ice floe with his dying beloved, realises that all the magic in the world cannot replace one single moment of love, brought a tear to my eye. *Ivan the Terrible* is a runaway winner in romance.' I turned to shoot daggers at Viola, who was being congratulated by the banshees and didn't even look at me.

But Mrs Parsing was still booming on.

'Marvellous jokes, lovely title, and that deliciously absurd ending' – here Mrs Parsing broke off to chuckle richly to herself – 'and I loved your technique of leaving in all the little notes in brackets. Altogether a most sophisticated parody of someone desperate to write a romance and going wonderfully over the top. *The Lady of the Rings* was the sure-fire winner in the comedy section. You really do have the makings of a fine comedy writer, Cordelia.'

What?! I'd won comedy? Hoodies and banshees descended on me with congratulations. 'Keep it up. Keep it up, all of you,' Mrs Parsing boomed on. 'I will be sitting the three of you together for English next term, so you can bounce ideas off each other.' And off she swooped, leaving me doing my Blue impression and Viola smiling a subtle smile.

I turned to her. I looked at her searchingly. Emotions were scudding across her face all right, but I couldn't make them out.

'Brilliant, isn't it?' she said. 'BOTH of us winning!'

'Sure,' I said. And left. I knew what the scudding emotion was as I turned away. Misery. But I was too miserable to care. I couldn't believe that Viola had taken my story out of the romance section so that she could win it. Obviously someone else must have found it wherever she hid it and tossed it back on to the wrong pile. But I also couldn't work out what Mrs Parsing meant by little notes in *The Lady of the Rings*. A dreadful suspicion began to dawn on me . . .

I ransacked my room the minute I got back home. It didn't take long, even amid the usual chaos of books, inks, pens, stationery, chocolate wrappers and recent vast piles of Kleenex to unearth another, identical pink folder, with 'rough version' scrawled across its cover. Inside, was not the rough version at all. Instead, it was the beautifully computer-generated, double-spaced, final version of *The Lady of the Rings*, without a single note and with lots of the over the top stuff honed down. How could I have put them in the wrong folders?

I felt hot and sticky at the thought of Mrs Parsing reading my scrawly rough with all my daft jokes in (highlights of which is, of course, the very same version that you have just read, Dear Reader, in this very same book that you are hold-ing now).

I realised that I'd been so tired that evening when I fin-ished it. Knackered, what with the *Home Alone* plot, the glue and feathers fiasco and the emotional overload of Callum's life, first in ruins and then miraculously repaired. And the next morning I had got the dreaded lurgy . . .

I re-read my 'best' version of *The Lady of the Rings*.

'Golden curls which normally grew all down her back.' Gadzooks. And more. And more. I realised that even my best version was so over the top as to be quite funny too. Like an example of bad writing, really, if I was honest.

Would Mrs Parsing have found this version almost as funny? Am I destined to be a comic writer?

Laura Hunt's Top Tips for Budding Writers:

Be prepared for rejection. In sport, not everyone will win. In friendship, not everyone will want to be your friend. In writing, not every publisher will love your book. Even if your book is published, not every reader will enjoy it.

Great. Is Aunt Laura actually trying to encourage us budding talents or not?

I had to write to Aunt Laura, to pretend to myself it was all OK.

Dear Aunt Laura,

I have won first prize in the school writing competition! I am on my way to becoming famous! Like you! They are sending my story in to the local paper. I decided my romance would work better as a short comedy. I realised that my style is actually more suited to parody, although I intend to pursue my creative vision of romance in later volumes. And so I have won the comic section. Isn't that amazing?!

Have you ever tried to write comedy? No offence, I know some of your books are funny in places, but mostly they are addressing rather sad issues. But in the little bits where they are funny did you start out thinking of comedy, or did those bits just turn out that way? I would like to enter a story for the romance section in next year's competition and I wonder if you have any tips. I imagine you don't have to read much to write children's books, especially ones that are about miserable families and so on because you can learn about those things from magazines and TV, can't you? To be honest, I would most like to be a proper writer for adults and win the Booker prize. So, now I am truly 'on my way' I would really appreciate some more top tips from you.

I am enclosing two fake birds for the Joans. They are for 'animal-loving pet owners'. I'm not sure what kind of pet owners hate animals but that's advertising for you. They smell of real birds, so since the Joans can't wear their bells, they might have fun ripping these apart instead.
Loads of love,
Cordelia xoxo

But what I really wanted to write was, 'Are comedy writers as good as real serious writers? It seems to me that everyone likes tragic, deep, soulful stuff and that is what I prefer. Could I be taken seriously if I was a comedy writer? And could I earn a living from it? And can you put your heart and soul and the very essence of your being into comedy?

And **HAVE YOU EVER HAD A FRIEND THAT YOU THOUGHT WAS A TRUE FRIEND BUT SHE BETRAYED YOU?!**'

But I didn't write that bit. I licked the envelope and sloped miserably off downstairs. On the doormat was a scrawled note, folded in half, and addressed to me.

> *Sorry, sorry, sorry. I know I shouldn't have, but I couldn't resist reading a bit of your fantastic story before I handed it in. I realised it was your rough version and after I had put it in the pile of entries for romance I kept thinking and worrying about it all day. I tried to phone you, but your mum said you were asleep so I had to make a decision fast. I just knew it would win comedy – what with all those notes to yourself and your natural wit, which shines through in everything you do – so I swapped it round and put it on the comedy pile. I did it to help you, honestly, and I NEVER, for ONE MINUTE, thought I would win romance. Will you ever forgive me?*
> *V*
> *P.S. You rushed off so quick you didn't see Mrs Warren coming in to say she was very proud of us both and that she would 'have the hags flung out'. I don't think she was referring to the banshees, I think she probably meant 'have the flags hung out'.*

Then ye bright sunrise of troth broke through ye grey deceptive dawne of misunderstanding. Viola had realised my story was funny and I hadn't. She did it to help me. And it'll be in the local paper, so that's good. I've started my journey as a writer, that's what counts.

I'll have to tell Viola I know her secret. She's kept mine about Aunt Laura and I can keep hers about her dad. And I'll make sure Tobylerone and Snort will keep it too. I realise Viola hasn't told me anything about herself, but I also realise I haven't tried very hard to find out. Everything's been all about me. Maybe, and I really hate to admit this, at the back of my mind I've been thinking Candice will disapprove of Viola if she knows she's a bit 'rough'. I do hope her dad's not inside for murder. I've got to find out more so I can help her. Probably he's innocent and it's all a miscarriage of justice. Or could Tobylerone have made it up? I'd like to think so, but I doubt it. I've also realised you can't judge a dude by his hoodie because I think Snort and Tobylerone have turned out to be really cool. And, I hate to admit it, but Zandra and Jolene gave me some chewing gum and said 'good on you' when they heard I won comedy. I have been a snob. I am going to have a word with Candice about all this. First step is going to be calling her and Howard Mum and Dad.

Still don't know how I feel about comedy, though. No one takes it seriously, do they? I realise I've got a lot to learn, but I'm determined to do it.

I think I'll try a detective novel next. *Girl Writer Volume* II: *The Secret of the Scorched Shirts of Doome.* Or maybe *The Prisoner of Falmer.*

Gadzooks, got to go and buy a friend for Blue. Maybe I'll get a woman goldfish and call it Pink and they can have some little mauve tadpoles or whatever it is that goldfish have.

But first, I must phone Viola. And together, we'll free her dad.

YE ENDE

P.S. Did you spot ye pangram?
And ye palindrome?
And Mrs Warren's spoonerisms?

www.piccadillypress.co.uk

★ The latest news on forthcoming books

★ Chapter previews

★ Author biographies

★ Fun quizzes

★ Reader reviews

★ Competitions and fab prizes

★ Book features and cool downloads

★ And much, much more . . .

Log on and check it out!

Piccadilly Press

★